DAY OF THE WED
ANNABELLE ARCHER WEDDING PLANNER MYSTERY
BOOK NINETEEN

LAURA DURHAM

BROADMOOR BOOKS

This book is dedicated to my wonderful readers! Thank you for your sweet messages, lovely reviews, and endless patience!

CHAPTER 1

"Will you look at that view?" I stepped from the van, stretching my stiff legs, and putting a hand over my eyes as I peered at the blue sea that stretched endlessly into the distance. I breathed in the salty air and shrugged off my cardigan, which had been helpful on the plane but was too warm for Mexico, even though it was almost November.

"Will you look at these wrinkles?" My best friend Richard joined me, but he wasn't appreciating the view of the Caribbean. His eyes were firmly trained on the creases in his beige linen shirt as he let out a long-suffering sigh.

Kate hopped from the other side of the car and bounced over to us, her blonde bob swinging. She barely glanced at Richard. "It's linen. What did you expect?"

Richard narrowed his eyes at her. "If there's anyone who understands linen, it's me." He flicked his fingers through his dark, choppy hair. "This is a linen blend that is supposed to be ideal for traveling, although maybe it isn't designed to withstand a plane, two taxis, and a ferry ride."

"Then maybe someone shouldn't have suggested we move the bachelorette festivities from the all-inclusive resort on the Riviera Maya to a sleepy little Mexican island." Fern was the last to emerge from the van, his hot-pink airplane pillow still hooked around his neck like an inflatable necklace as he yawned widely. His dark hair was pulled up into a high man bun, which highlighted the fact that DC's top wedding hairstylist looked like Errol Flynn without the mustache.

"Isla Mujeres isn't a sleepy little island," Richard said indignantly. "I'll have you know that this island is quickly becoming an elite destination for those who love Mexico without all the abominable tourists."

"Aren't we tourists?" Kate said to me from the side of her mouth.

"We don't count." Richard hoisted a black Prada carry-on bag onto his shoulder. "We're integrating with the community, which is something we couldn't have done in one of those all-inclusive monstrosities."

Fern swiveled his head to take in the long road we'd arrived on, which hugged the coastline of the island that was dotted with private homes overlooking the water, each more impressive than the next. "The locals live here? I thought we got this house because of your connection to a DC socialite."

Richard frowned, shifting from one foot to the other. "Gail and her husband have been coming here so long they're practically locals."

Fern smirked at me then squinted at the expansive house with a traditional thatched roof and mango-colored exterior perched at the end of the sloping drive. It had clearly been designed to look like it was native to the island while also being larger than any local home would ever be. "I'll admit the house is charming, and the view is spectacular."

"Of course it is, although I don't know if a five-bedroom house with a private pool can be called charming," Richard said.

"Whatever it is, it's ours for the next few days." Kate threw an arm around my shoulders. "I plan to spend those days eating, sunning, and drinking too many margaritas." When she spotted Richard's disapproving look, she gave him one of her own. "It is my bachelorette party, after all. You didn't think we were coming here to do juice cleanses and cultural tours, did you?"

Richard muttered something about a juice cleanse doing her liver good, but Kate ignored him.

"I might not be able to drink with you," I said, "but that doesn't mean this can't be the best bachelorette celebration ever."

Kate squeezed my shoulders. "You can't help being pregnant. Besides, it will be nice to have someone else throwing up for once."

"Let's hope that part of the pregnancy is behind me." I touched a hand to my baby bump which, at a little over five months, had just started to be noticeable.

For the first trimester, I hadn't been able to even think of fish without turning green, which had made my job as the head of Wedding Belles, Washington DC's premier wedding planning company, more challenging than usual. Luckily, my newly minted business partner, Kate, had been right by my side handling any tasting involving salmon and taking point position when it came to raw bars. I'd made it through the summer wedding season with only mild morning sickness, although I was pretty sure my ability to smell could rival that of a bomb-sniffing dog.

Richard patted his designer carry-on. "Don't worry about a thing, Annabelle. I packed all the pregnancy essentials to make sure this trip is perfectly safe."

I eyed his bag, which was usually filled with designer clothes and skin care products. "You did?"

He gave me a disdainful look. "What kind of future godfather would let you travel internationally without being fully prepared? I assured Reese that I would watch you like a hawk and make sure you took your prenatal vitamins and hydrated properly."

I tried not to groan aloud at the thought of being watched like a hawk. "I'll have to give my darling husband a call and thank him for making you his proxy worrywart."

Since I'd discovered I was pregnant a bit earlier than we'd planned, I'd seen an entirely new side to my husband. Even though he was a detective with the DC police force, he'd always been the more laid back of the two of us—until now. Mike had swung into full protective mode, refusing to let me carry anything up to our fourth-floor walk-up, even if it was only a bag of groceries, and taking over shopping so that he could ensure we had healthy food in the apartment, something I'd admittedly never been great at doing. Gone were the days of me chugging a Mocha Frappuccino in place of a meal or eating leftover take-out Thai for three days. I'd known he'd roped my friends into his neurotic fussing since they now took any bag or box from my arms without asking, but I hadn't been aware that Richard had been tasked with taking over the obsessive worrying on Mike's behalf for the duration of Kate's bachelorette celebration.

Richard flapped a hand at me, missing my sarcasm. "No need to thank me. The pleasure is all mine. What are best friends for?"

Since Richard had decided that he was also my husband's best friend, I wasn't sure which one of us he meant.

"As long as the Reese brothers are only here in spirit," Fern said. "As hunky as they both are, having the groom-to-be at the bachelorette party is a buzz kill."

I was still adjusting to the fact that my long-time assistant and now business partner was engaged to my husband's older brother, Daniel. Kate had always been a serial dater with a black book that could rival Casanova's, but the slightly older and more serious Reese brother had managed to capture her heart right under our noses.

Kate swatted playfully at Fern. "My fiancé could never be a buzz kill, but it is fun to have some time without the boys."

Richard cleared his throat.

"You know what I mean," Kate said. "The type of boys who like to watch sports and drink beer."

Both Richard and Fern shuddered, and even I was glad the men on our trip were more interested in finger bowls than Super Bowls.

"Why don't we settle into the house before the rest of the group arrives?" I said, twisting my neck to see that our driver had unloaded all of our suitcases from the back of the van.

Fern whipped off his airplane pillow. "I almost forgot that Leatrice and the Mighty Morphin Flower Arrangers aren't arriving until later."

"I don't know how you missed that," Richard muttered.

"I hope that isn't a comment on Buster's and Mack's notable appearance," I said, giving Richard the stink eye. My go-to florists were also husky Christian bikers who wore head-to-

toe black leather and sported bald heads, goatees, and piercings.

"Buster and Mack?" He pressed a hand to his heart. "You wound me, Annabelle. I meant that the flight was blessedly quiet because Leatrice wasn't on it."

"Oh." I couldn't argue with the fact that my octogenarian neighbor was prone to nonstop chatter.

"I, for one, can't wait for the old gal to arrive," Fern said, grabbing his rolling suitcase and bumping it down the pebbled drive. "She said she found matching PJs for all of us."

"Heaven preserve us," Richard said under his breath as we all followed Fern down the drive toward the house. Leatrice was also known for her bold fashion choices, none of which Richard appreciated.

We all pulled our wheeled luggage behind us, although Richard insisted on dragging mine, as well, and he stopped every few feet to readjust his hands and complain.

"I *can* pull a suitcase," I told him, slowing down to match his slower pace as Kate and Fern disappeared into the house.

He huffed out a breath. "Not on my watch." Then he paused. "Do you think I'm doing the right thing, darling?"

"By dragging two suitcases?"

He gave me a disdainful look. "No, by leaving Hermès with Sidney Allen?"

After being a self-proclaimed avoider of pets or children for his entire life, Richard had fallen hard for his partner's Yorkie, renaming him Hermès and carrying him around in his man bag. When he had to leave the energetic dog behind, Leatrice usually babysat. Despite Richard's complaints that she didn't feed him entirely organic food, and she put ribbons in his fur that didn't match the dog's aesthetic, he did trust her. Now that Leatrice was joining us on the trip, he'd agreed to leave the Yorkie in the hands of Leatrice's husband, Sidney Allen.

"At least you can be sure that he won't put Hermès in matching PJs."

Richard sucked in air. "If I come home and Hermès is wearing pants to his chin like Sidney Allen, I will die."

"He won't put your dog in pants. Besides, I asked my husband to check in on them." The reality was that Sidney Allen would probably show up with Hermès in tow before Mike could even attempt to check in on them. The rotund entertainment director had acquired the same bad habit as his wife of popping in unannounced and staying.

"That makes me feel better," Richard said, resuming our trek and kicking up pebbles in the wake of both suitcases.

We finally made it inside the house, stepping into a great room with a soaring ceiling that overlooked a patio and an infinity pool that disappeared into the sea. Fern and Kate were already standing under the white pergola on the pool deck that was draped with fabric that blew in the breeze.

Richard and I walked through the tastefully appointed room and through the open glass sliding door to join our friends.

"Now this is a view I can get used to," Kate said, glancing to the bar set up to one side. "Especially if that bar is stocked."

"Should I whip up a batch of cocktails?" Fern walked toward the bar without waiting for a reply, although he gave me a sympathetic look over his shoulder. "And a mocktail for you, sweetie."

Before I could tell him that a mocktail sounded perfect, a piercing voice shattered the calm.

"Don't think I won't call the police on you!"

CHAPTER 2

"Who was that?" Richard spun around, whipping his head from side to side.

There was no one but us on the pool deck or in the house, but the voice had sounded close enough to make the hairs on the back of my neck stand on end. "I'm not sure, but they aren't happy."

"If you think you can bully me out of my house, you don't know me very well!"

This time I was able to pinpoint the screeching voice. I nudged Kate in the ribs. "It's coming from the house next door."

We all swiveled our heads to see a platinum blonde strutting back and forth in front of her own pool, her white maxi dress swirling around her ankles. She held a phone to her ear while she gestured with her free hand.

Richard frowned. "That must be the neighbor Gail mentioned."

We all pivoted to him with expectant expressions.

He released a breath as if he were under grave duress. "Fine. My friend might have mentioned the crazy neighbor who's going through a nasty divorce and fighting over their vacation home."

I gave Richard a pointed look. "And you didn't mention this to us?"

He waved a hand in the air, doing a spot-on impersonation of the neighbor's flailing hand as she yelled into her phone. "I thought Gail was exaggerating, and I hoped that Marla had mellowed out over the years."

"Marla?" Kate cut her gaze to the neighbor. "Does this mean you actually know her?"

Richard shifted from one foot to the other, not meeting our eyes. "Know *of* her is more like it. She's from DC, but I've never worked for her." He made a face. "I used to work for the first Mrs. Bottinger, but when Marla arrived, she got rid of everything with any connection to the first wife. I was out. I have no idea who's done her parties for the past decade but I'm sure they've been just as tacky and nouveau riche as she is."

"Tell us what you really think," Fern murmured, glancing quickly at the woman before tapping one finger on his chin. "Marla Bottinger? She's not one of my rich tramps, but I can tell you she's not a real blonde, and she needs her roots done."

"So, is your friend Gail friends with this Marla?" I asked.

"Not exactly," Richard said. "Gail was tight with the first Mrs. B. I think that's how they both ended up with houses down here next to each other, although I also remember her saying something about how the house couldn't go to her friend during the first divorce because of some specific rule on the island about property ownership." He cocked his head as if trying to remember the details. "I do think she said the original Mrs. B remarried and has her own vacation home down here, a bigger and even better one."

Fern produced a couple of bottles from under the bar. "Maybe we should suggest that strategy to wife number two."

The woman continued to scream into the phone about not leaving the house unless it was feet first, finally jamming a finger at the screen to disconnect and throwing the phone onto a nearby lounge chair. Then she looked up, seeming to realize for the first time that she had an audience. She blanched before jutting her chin into the air. "You aren't Gail."

Kate gave Marla a cheery wave. "We're friends of hers down for a few days to celebrate my bachelorette. I'm Kate and this is Annabelle, Richard, and Fern."

"Marla," the woman replied, unable to maintain her anger in the face of Kate's bubbly personality, although her voice didn't hold much warmth. "I'm Gail's neighbor—for now."

"We'll try to keep things down," Kate continued. "We're not planning a wild time"

Marla shrugged. "Then you picked the wrong time to come to Isla. It's almost the Day of the Dead."

We'd noticed lots of skeletons in fancy dress and brightly painted skulls in the small downtown when we'd arrived, but I hadn't given it much thought.

"Of course," Richard said to himself. "How could I have forgotten?"

I patted his arm. "It's been a crazy wedding season. I think we've all lost track of days and weeks as we've gone from wedding to wedding every weekend this fall."

"What's the Day of the Dead?" Kate asked.

"Only one of the biggest celebrations of the year in Mexico." Richard scraped a hand through his hair. "It takes place on November the first, but the parties and parades go on for days. The graveyards are packed with families gathering to celebrate those who've died. They eat and drink and party at the graves."

Fern looked up from the drinks he was mixing. "I've never been to a party at a graveyard."

"If you were hoping for a peaceful time, I'm afraid you're not going to get it," Marla said, picking up one of the many half-empty glasses littering the side tables around the pool.

"Are you here for the celebrations?" Kate asked.

Marla's heavily made-up face contorted for a beat before she plastered a tight smile back on. "No. I'm in the middle of a divorce. I'm here because my soon-to-be ex is trying to take the house from me."

"How awful." Kate shook her head, although I knew from her tone of voice that she wasn't being sincere.

Luckily, Marla didn't know Kate or the placating tones she used to pry information from people. "If he thinks I'm going to roll over just because he has fancier lawyers and he speaks Spanish, he's in for a shock. I've been spending my summers here for almost a decade. I'm not giving it up so he can move *her* in here."

I assumed "her" was the new woman in her ex's life, although I wasn't about to ask.

"How do you spend a decade of summers here and not pick up Spanish?" Richard whispered to me as he made a point of turning his head.

"*No se*," I answered him, putting to use the rudimentary Spanish skills I'd acquired from an app I'd started using a few weeks ago.

"*Bien*, Annabelle," he replied with a grin.

"Since you're here, you might as well join in the fun," Marla said. "Even if you don't care about the festival, you can dress up and have a good time. I always put on a fancy Mexican dress and go downtown."

The bottle blonde didn't strike me as someone who was worried about offending others or turning a beloved cultural ritual into an excuse for a party, but I also doubted she was alone.

"Thanks for the tips," Kate called out. "I'm sure we'll see you around."

Marla gave us a final wave as she scooped up her phone and retreated into her multilevel, white stucco house with glass walls facing the ocean. With the beachfront location and stunning views, I understood why she was eager to keep the house.

Fern waved us toward a round table that sat underneath the roof overhang of the house and was shaded from the brutal sun. He'd already set out two drinks and he brought two more as we took seats.

I let out a grateful sigh to be off my feet and another one after I took a sip of the blue concoction Fern set in front of me. It was sweet and fruity, and best of all, cold.

"What's in these?" Kate asked as she kicked off her yellow, high-heeled mules and propped her long, bare legs on the empty chair next to her.

"A bit of everything," Fern said, then gave me a knowing smile. "And in yours, almost everything."

I twisted my rattan, swivel chair so it faced the ocean. "This is perfect, festival or no festival."

"I like the idea of being here during the Day of the Dead." Kate took a long sip of her drink. "I wouldn't mind checking out the parades and parties."

I leveled a finger at her. "But we're not dressing up."

She wrinkled her nose at me. "Of course not."

Fern's face fell. "Not even a little bit?" One of his favorite things was to dress according to the occasion. The chances of me keeping him from a costume were slim.

"You'll fit in more than Marla will," I admitted, taking in his dark hair and tan skin.

"How has she spent so much time here and never picked up the language?" Kate asked, shaking her head.

Richard shrugged. "From what I remember, Mr. Bottinger did not marry Marla for her brains. The first wife was the one he married before he made all his money in government contracting. Then he got some money and upgraded everything."

"And now he's trading her in for a younger model," Fern said. "Why do these bimbos never learn that what comes around, goes around?"

Kate raised her glass. "I think we've already said she isn't the sharpest wife in the drawer."

Richard exchanged a glance with me. Normally Kate mangled expressions, but this time her malaprop seemed to work.

"If the lady wasn't so foolish, she wouldn't bring her lovers to her husband's house."

For the second time that day, we all searched for the source of the accented voice, but this time it didn't come from a brassy blonde. It came from a small woman standing inside the open sliding glass door and wearing an apron.

CHAPTER 3

"Never let it be said that Fern isn't eager for someone to spill the tea, but who are you, sweetie?" He touched a hand to his immaculate hair as he eyed the woman who wiped her hands nervously on the front of her apron.

"I'm Carlita. I take care of the house." She glanced to one side as a man a bit taller than her appeared from the side of the house and walked toward the pool. "Along with my husband, who takes care of the pool and grounds."

Richard jumped to his feet. "Gail mentioned you and said you were a godsend, but you don't have to worry about taking care of the house while we're here. I promised Gail we'd leave the house so clean there would be no trace of us."

Carlita smiled but shook her head. "I will come." Then she cut her gaze to the side of the house that abutted Marla's. "I have to come for Mrs. B anyway."

Fern let out a breath. "Finally, we're back to the important part. You said something about Marla and lovers?"

Carlita's eyes dropped. "I shouldn't have said anything. I was frustrated."

Fern stood and walked to the woman, putting an arm around her shoulders and steering her toward the table. "You don't ever need to apologize to us. Now tell me more about these lovers. There was more than one?"

Carlita snorted out a laugh then slapped a hand over her mouth. "I'm sorry. It's just funny to think of Mrs. B with only one lover."

Kate leaned forward and put her elbows on the glass tabletop. "How does she bring them to the house without her husband knowing?"

"I think there's a reason they're getting divorced," Fern muttered.

"If he already has a new girlfriend, I'm assuming the infidelity isn't new or one-sided," I added, although I was always surprised when people chose to bring lovers to their homes. Hadn't they watched enough movies where spouses had come home early to know not to make that mistake?

Carlita pressed her lips together until they were a white line. "Mrs. B has been bringing lovers for a long time, but her husband rarely comes to the house anymore, so it isn't my place to say anything."

"Have you been working for the family for a long time?" Richard asked. "Gail said you'd been with her since they got the house."

Carlita bobbed her head up and down. "I started with the first Mrs. B. Now she is a nice lady to work for." She shot another murderous glance at the wall closest to the neighboring house.

"Nothing like this one." Then she smiled at Richard. "Your friend is also a nice lady."

"She was friends with the first wife," Richard said. "I catered parties at the Bottinger house for years before they divorced. It's how I met Gail. She and Brenda were best friends." His brow furrowed. "I wonder how she didn't know about all Marla's affairs."

"Mrs. B hides them when your friend comes, which isn't as often anymore." Carlita dropped her voice as if Marla could hear through the walls. "Then she pretends to be the lonely wife."

"Maybe Marla is the reason Gail stopped using this house as much," Richard said. "Who would want to be next door to the woman who stole your best friend's husband?"

Kate held up two sets of crossed fingers. "Fingers crossed the third wife is better."

Carlita released a weary sigh and took a step back. "I should get back to work. Mrs. B will be expecting me, and she doesn't tolerate lateness."

We watched as the woman slipped back inside.

"Mrs. B sounds like a huge B," Kate said. "And a floozy, to steal one of Fern's favorite terms for bridesmaids."

Fern inclined his head to her in acknowledgment then rubbed his hands together. "This is so tawdry. I love it."

"We're supposed to be celebrating Kate's impending marriage," I said, "not relishing in the disintegration of someone else's."

"Don't worry, sweetie." Fern gave me a wink. "I'm a champion multitasker. I can celebrate Kate's wedding and enjoy a society second marriage falling apart."

DAY OF THE WED

Kate held up a finger. "And we aren't celebrating my marriage. We're celebrating my final days as a single woman."

"That's right." Fern's face brightened. "In that case, a sex scandal fits right in."

"Thanks." Kate made a face. "I think."

"As delightful as it is to fly all the way from Washington DC to talk about some socialites from the city, we are officially in the Caribbean," Richard said. "I promised Reese I'd make sure his pregnant wife got some rest after a hectic wedding season, which does not mean getting involved in the tawdry affairs of the second Mrs. Bottinger."

Fern muttered something about Richard being a spoilsport, but Kate drained the last of her drink. "R.G. is right. We're here to have fun and unwind, which means no DC divas or drama."

I cocked an eyebrow at her. If that was the rule, then we'd brought the wrong crew. Fern and Richard were both divas who gravitated toward drama like moths to flames.

"R.G.?" Richard asked. "Is that short for Richard Gerard? You know how I loathe nicknames."

She grinned and nodded. "I know."

Before things went completely off the rails and the two started sniping at each other, I held up my palms. "Why don't we pick bedrooms and unpack? The rest of our crew will be here by this evening."

"Good thinking." Richard glanced at his Gucci watch. "Annabelle, you could use a nap. Reese said you need to get more sleep than you've been getting."

I fought the urge to roll my eyes and tell him that I wasn't a child and didn't need a nap, but as soon as he said it, I was struck with the irrepressible desire to yawn. Maybe a nap wasn't such a bad idea. It had been an early morning flight, which had meant we'd been at the airport at the crack of dawn.

"We're sharing rooms, aren't we?" I asked after stifling my yawn. "At least some of us?"

"I thought we could give Buster and Mack the guesthouse," Richard said, swinging into the bossy persona that made him such an effective head of DC's most exclusive catering company. "I've heard them snore before, and trust me, none of us are sleeping through that."

"There's a guesthouse?" Kate asked.

Richard nodded, already moving efficiently toward the luggage we'd all left sitting in the entrance of the great room. "It's right next to the main house and shares a roof, but it has its own entrance."

"And, let's hope, thicker walls," I said under my breath since I'd heard the two burly men snore before too.

"Kate should have her own room since she's the guest of honor," Fern said.

Richard frowned at this. "That means that you're bunking with Leatrice because Annabelle should have her own room."

Fern did the mental math. "Doesn't that mean you also get your own room?"

Richard shot Fern a look. "If you want Leatrice to leave this celebration alive, you won't put her in the same room as me."

"I don't know what you're talking about." Fern hooked his pink airplane pillow around his neck again and grabbed his suitcase. "Leatrice is a hoot and a half. Our room is going to be the fun room."

Richard directed us all to our rooms, which were spread out on both sides of the house presumably, so they all had Caribbean views. My room was next to his, and I knew it was no accident that Fern, Leatrice, and Kate were on the other side. I'd just stepped into the room he'd assigned me and appraised the neatly made queen-size bed and the decor in subtle shades of beige and sea green when there was a loud noise from the great room followed by a series of thuds and thunks.

"Guess who!"

CHAPTER 4

"I thought they were coming later," Richard said in a stage whisper as we gathered in front of the house to leave for dinner. "You promised me we had almost an entire day before she arrived."

I elbowed him. It was too late to tell him to lower his voice, but luckily Leatrice was too distracted by our decision to go downtown for an early dinner and the adventure of using the house's provided golf carts for the first time.

"We were able to catch an earlier flight," Buster said, readjusting the motorcycle goggles that perched on top of his bald head and seemingly undisturbed that Richard was complaining about their early arrival.

Mack gave us a bright smile over our shoulder. "Our bridal consultation was a no-show, so we closed the shop early, swung by and picked up Leatrice, and sweet-talked the airline ladies into switching us to an earlier flight."

"That's right." Leatrice bobbed her head enthusiastically, her jet-black Mary Tyler Moore flip barely moving. "I'd wanted to spend a little more time with my sugar muffin before we left, but he had to put out some fires for an upcoming event. Halloween is a big season for bespoke entertainment and costumed performers, you know."

Leatrice's sugar muffin, Sidney Allen, owned an entertainment company that specialized in providing costumed performers dressed as anything from Dickens-style carolers at Christmas to political impersonators for fundraisers. The two had met when Leatrice had crashed one of my weddings where Sidney Allen had provided the Carnival-themed performers, and the two little misfit toys had been inseparable ever since.

"He's not too busy to properly supervise Hermès, is he?" Richard asked, promptly forgetting about being upset that Leatrice had arrived early.

"Not at all." Leatrice flapped a bony hand in our general direction. "He incorporated Hermès's schedule into his event timelines for the next few days, so he won't forget feedings or walks."

Richard blinked a few times. "He did? That's brilliant. Why haven't I thought of that before?" He nudged me. "We should do that when Little Richard arrives."

"Little Richard?" Kate's eyebrows shot up so high they were in danger of leaving her forehead.

"We are *not* calling the baby Little Richard," I said as Kate's shoulders started to shake, and she clamped a hand over her mouth. "We don't even know if it's a boy or a girl."

Richard held up a finger. "That's another bone I have to pick with you, Annabelle. We need to know the sex of the baby so we can work on the nursery."

"You mean the office slash nursery?" Kate gave me a look, which I tried to ignore. The only spare room for the baby was the current Wedding Belles office, and Kate had been arguing for a separate office space or a bigger apartment for my growing family. "I hope your baby doesn't mind playing with wedding favors as toys."

"The baby won't be big enough to play with anything for months," I said. "I still have time to figure out a solution."

I was saved from more of Richard's bones to pick by Fern swooping up to us in a golf cart. "Here's the first one." He jerked a thumb behind him. "There's one more in the garage."

Mack lumbered off in the direction of the garage, his black leather pants creaking as he walked. "I'll get it."

Kate jumped into Fern's golf cart. "I love that the island's small enough to use golf carts for transportation. This is going to be fun!"

I'd witnessed Fern driving a golf cart before, and although his speed and eventual crash had been because he'd been in pursuit of an escaping killer, I decided to ride with Mack. Luckily, Leatrice had never seen Fern captain a golf cart, so she hopped onto the back, her multicolored peasant skirt jingling.

Mack pulled up behind Fern's cart, and Buster, Richard and I all hurried to get on. Buster insisted I take the front passenger seat next to Mack, partially to be chivalrous, but also because the two husky men couldn't fit side by side in the compact cart. As it was, Richard and I both were shoulder to shoulder with the leather-clad florists.

With a beep of his horn, Fern's cart lurched forward, and we followed, driving down the road that skirted the ocean as the sun sank farther toward the horizon. I gripped the overhead bar tightly, even though we were driving well below the speed limit, taking in the houses fronting the water—including one shaped like a standing conch shell—and eyeing the graveyard on our left with its colorful aboveground crypts topped with crosses reaching for the sky.

As we approached the town, we encountered traffic—cars and fellow golf carts—along with tourists walking along the side of the road. Restaurants were open with tables set up on patios, and souvenir shops proudly displayed garish T-shirts, ornate sugar skulls, and elaborate costumes. The scent of salt in the air was overpowered by the savory aroma of food, and the raucous laughter spilling from doorways told me that the tequila was already flowing freely.

Fern swerved into a parking spot on the street, leaving enough room for us to pull in beside him. Mack parked carefully and turned off the engine.

Buster stepped down and inhaled deeply. "If I wasn't hungry before, I am now."

My stomach growled, reminding me that I hadn't eaten since the meager cookies offered on the plane and the protein bar Richard had insisted I eat on the ferry. Now that I thought about it, I was ravenous.

"Gail recommended Rolandi's," Richard said, peering at his phone and pointing vaguely in front of us. "It should be down this street."

"Rolandi's?" Fern wrinkled his nose as he smoothed the front of his white guayabera shirt with matching embroidery on the front. "That doesn't sound Mexican."

"It's Italian," Richard said as he walked forward with purpose. "Gail swears by the pasta."

Fern muttered something about looking forward to trying the tacos in Rome, but Richard was too far ahead of him to catch it.

"As long as it's edible," I said.

Kate looped her arm through mine as we walked. "Let's get some food in this baby bump."

The downtown of the island wasn't more than a few streets lined with three-story buildings made from gray concrete occasionally painted pale blue or salmon pink and fronted with fabric awnings.

Richard paused in front of a melon-colored building with windows above the peaked awning and small balconies with iron railings. Gold letters spelling out Rolandi's ran in a vertical line down the length of the building, and a blue awning proclaimed that we'd found Rolandi's and that they served Corona beer.

Richard held up seven fingers, and a host ushered us inside the restaurant. After passing through the brick archway, I was startled to find that the interior of the restaurant had been designed to look like an outdoor courtyard. White string lights were strung across a large, open room that rose three stories and had balconies, windows, and a staircase that ran up the side of one wall. Plants spilled from windows and vines crisscrossed the open space. A traditional tiled fountain sat under the stairs, and wooden wagon wheels hung on the walls.

We were led to a long, rectangular table made by pushing together three smaller tables, and we each took one of the chunky, fabric-backed wooden chairs. Inside the restaurant, the aroma from the wood-burning pizza oven made me almost light-headed, and I gratefully took the thick menu.

As Fern ordered a round of margaritas for the table and a lemonade for me, I studied the expansive menu and hoped the cooks didn't operate on island time.

Mack jumped when his phone trilled in his pocket and stood to wiggle the device from his leather pants. He beamed when he saw the name on the screen. "It's Prue. I told her to call me before she put Merry to bed so we could sing to her."

Richard eyed the man. "Sing to her?"

Buster stood up next to Mack. "She's used to us singing lullabies to her each night. I'm afraid she has a hard time getting to sleep without them."

"We'll take this outside," Mack said as he answered and headed for the restaurant's entrance with Buster close behind him.

"I wonder if they'd sing me to sleep," Leatrice said.

I imagined the two men's deep, growly voices could be very soothing—or terrifying.

Richard sucked in a breath, but before I could warn him not to rag on our friends' singing ability, I glanced up at him. He was sitting directly across from me facing the entrance to the restaurant shaking his head. "Impossible."

"What's impossible? Two grown men singing to their practically adopted baby daughter from a country away?"

"That even in Mexico they put pineapple on pizza?" Fern muttered as he read the menu.

"No." Richard leaned over and grasped my hand. "I think I just saw Mr. Bottinger."

It took me a beat to make the connection. "You mean the soon-to-be ex-husband of our screeching neighbor?" I craned my neck over my shoulder but only saw the retreating back of a tall man.

"So much for us seeing the last of Marla's drama," Richard said. "And unless my eyes were playing tricks on me, her ex has his new girlfriend with him."

CHAPTER 5

"You saw Mr. who?" Leatrice asked as she followed me into the house with Richard bringing up the rear.

"I didn't see him." I dropped my purse into the nearest chair, which was white, modern, and armless, before lowering myself into a chair that did have arms. "Not that I would know what the guy looked like anyway."

"*I* saw him," Richard said with a huff. Leatrice had spent most of our golf cart ride home with her head between us as she tried to listen from the backseat, so this wasn't the first time Richard was explaining himself. "To be fair, it's been years since I've seen the man. The last time I was in his home was when I catered for the first Mrs. B, but the man I saw leaving Rolandi's looked like a slightly older version of the man I remember."

Leatrice plopped down on the couch across from me, her skirt jingling. "What are the odds you'd see a former client on this little island?"

"Almost as slim as renting the house next door to the second wife he's in the process of divorcing," I said, knowing very well I was throwing gasoline onto the flame of Leatrice's love of juicy gossip.

She swung her head right and left, her eyes wide. "What?"

Richard flipped on the lights in the kitchen that opened onto the main room. Like the rest of the house's interior, it was white with beige accents and had a wooden countertop. He retrieved three aluminum bottles of water from the refrigerator and juggled them in his arms as he joined us in the great room.

He gave me a pointed look as he walked toward me, but I was enjoying myself too much to be abashed. If I couldn't drink at a bachelorette celebration, at least I could enjoy watching Leatrice pepper Richard with questions.

The rest of our group had opted to stay downtown for a few more margaritas before calling it a night, while I'd decided I needed sleep. Richard and Leatrice had both insisted on escorting me home, although I suspected Leatrice might be as tired as I was. She was a spunky old lady, but she was still in her eighties.

"As you probably know," Richard said, glancing at Leatrice, "I got this house from my friend and longtime client Gail. She was best friends with the first Mrs. Bottinger, which is why they ended up with vacation homes next door." He gestured with his head toward the other house. "The second wife, who incidentally was the woman Mr. B cheated on his first wife with, is now being divorced and is attempting to keep the house."

He took a breath after his explanation and handed me one of the aluminum water bottles which had blue and green swirls on the outside. "Your Momoa water, darling."

Leatrice gaped at him after hearing the rundown of the scandal then eyed the bottle he handed her. "Momoa water?"

"It's all Richard will drink," I said in a mock stage whisper. "It's Jason Momoa's personal brand of water, and it uses aluminum bottles instead of plastic."

Leatrice tilted her head to one side. "Jason Momoa. Isn't he that hunky young man who plays Aquaman?"

"You know Aquaman?" I'd never known my downstairs neighbor to be much of a popular culture buff. Sure, Perry Mason reruns and *Murder, She Wrote*, but DC Comics movies?

Leatrice twisted off the cap of her can of Mananalu water. "I like to keep up with what the kids are watching. Besides, I like a man with long hair like that Momoa boy."

"You do?" I nearly slipped off my chair. Her husband had barely enough hair for his comb-over.

She gave me a wry smile. "You forget that I was in my thirties during the '70s. I knew my fair share of boys with long hair." She giggled. "Perhaps more than my fair share, now that I think about it."

Richard goggled at Leatrice, but I laughed. Every time I assumed I knew everything about my eccentric neighbor, she startled me with some tidbit about her mysterious past.

"Then you and Richard have something in common," I told her, relishing the flush that darkened my best friend's cheeks and the outraged look he gave me. "Why do you think he insists on drinking Momoa water?"

"I do it because it's better for the environment," Richard spluttered. "Do you know how much pollution is caused by single-use plastics? I now get all my catering disposables made from bamboo and have banned Styrofoam from the Richard Gerard Catering premises."

"I'm teasing you," I said. "I agree with you about plastics." I took a swig of the water, which happened to be lightly flavored with passion fruit. "It doesn't hurt that the spokesman for the water also played a bare chested Dothraki."

Richard avoided my gaze. "I don't know what you're talking about."

"I do." Leatrice waved an arm in the air. "I tried to convince my honeybun to get Khal Drogo and Khaleesi costumes, but he didn't go for it."

Richard almost choked on a mouthful of water. "If this conversation turns to what you and Sidney Allen wear in private, I'm going to have to excuse myself."

Leatrice giggled and tucked her legs under her, prompting more skirt jingling. "Not in private. For Halloween. I always give out candy to trick-or-treaters, even though we don't have as many in our building as we used to, and I always dress up."

Considering Leatrice's fondness for unusual clothing and accessories, this didn't surprise me. What surprised me was the idea of Sidney Allen in a costume. Despite managing performers who wore elaborate costumes, I rarely saw him in anything but a dark suit with the pants tucked up nearly to his armpits.

Richard released a loud breath. "Thank heavens for that."

"But you're missing Halloween this year since you're down here with us," I said.

Leatrice shrugged. "A sacrifice worth making to witness Kate's last hurrah as a single woman."

"If it is her last hurrah," Richard said somewhat under his breath.

I pivoted toward him. "What do you mean?"

"I can't be the only one who's noticed that she's barely started to plan her wedding. Even this celebration was supposed to be months ago."

"Because we had an insanely busy wedding season. Whatever happened to July and August being slow?" I heard the defensiveness in my voice, which was odd since I knew he had a point. Kate had been slow to start the planning process, even though she claimed to be excited about her engagement. Maybe I was defensive because I'd been slow to plan my own wedding, so I understood what it was like to make a life-changing decision. After watching so many couples exchange vows, it was almost surreal to think of doing it yourself.

"I don't blame her," Richard said. "Daniel Reese might be a silver fox hunk, but our Kate has been flitting from man to man since I met her. Not only is this her first serious relationship since she started working for you, now she's engaged? It's a lot. I only hope she knows what she's doing. Marrying the boss's brother-in-law—or not marrying him—could make things pretty tricky."

I hadn't given too much thought to the dynamics of my longtime assistant becoming my sister-in-law, but Richard was right. If things went South, what would that mean for Wedding Belles and for the friendship I'd come to count as one of my closest?

I took a big gulp of my Momoa water, wishing it was something a lot stronger.

CHAPTER 6

I rolled over and squinted at the sun shining through the floor-to-ceiling windows. The bright sunlight reflected off the sea as the waves rolled in rhythmically toward the rocky shore. I'd clearly slept in and missed the sunrise by a lot, although I felt more rested than I had in months. I stretched my arms over my head and took a deep breath. There was something about the island air and island vibe that made it impossible to feel as stressed as I did back in DC

I finally swung my feet onto the floor, wiggling my toes on the woven rug that covered the Mexican tile floor. Now that I was up, I was ready for breakfast, although what I really longed for were the sugary, caffeinated Mocha Frappuccinos that my husband had convinced me were not great for the baby. He'd even gone so far as to not drink coffee in front of me anymore, but that didn't change the fact that I missed my caffeine fix.

Padding from my bedroom into the great room, I was surprised to see the large space empty. Was it possible I was the first person up, even though from the sun's position in the sky, I guessed it must be late morning?

Then I slid my gaze to the pool deck and spotted two figures sprawled out on padded lounge chairs.

"Good morning," I called out, as I stepped through the open sliding glass door and walked across the terrace toward them. "Are you up early, or is this where you landed after coming in last night?"

I hadn't waited up for the rest of our group to return, although I'd heard some giggling and shuffling sounds at some point after I'd gone to bed. From Fern's and Kate's prone positions, it was entirely possible that they'd slept on the loungers.

Fern slowly twisted his head to me, revealing a pale-white, featureless face. "We just came out and put on detoxifying sheet masks. It's step one of our spa-by-the-pool day."

I released a breath. That explained his face.

Kate tipped her head back, her face also covered in the opaque, wet paper mask. "Join us. Fern brought enough for everyone, although you probably don't need to worry about detoxing like we do."

"Rough night last night?" I asked, taking the lounge chair next to Kate's. Aside from the mask, she wore a black-and-white striped bikini that tied at the sides.

"Actually, we ended up only having a couple more drinks before we joined the people on the street who were already celebrating."

Fern bobbed his head, and his sheet mask slid down his face a bit. "The bands were so much fun, but we were told that tonight is the official parade from the cemetery to the cultural center where they'll have more singing and dancing and displays of altars."

"So, we'll chill out and detox this morning to be ready for tonight," Kate winked at me from behind the ghoulish white mask that only had holes for her eyes, mouth, and nose.

Fern sat up while he kept his head back, digging with one hand in the bag next to his chair without looking. He produced a flat, shiny packet and handed it to me. "This should be a nourishing mask, which is perfect for you since that baby is probably sucking you dry."

"Pretty," Richard said, stepping from the house and wrinkling his nose. He held up a brown paper bag. "I brought breakfast."

My stomach rumbled, and I marveled at how I seemed to be hungry all the time. "You went out already?"

He smirked at me as he pivoted and headed back inside to the kitchen. "Not all of us can sleep until noon, darling."

I followed him, marveling at the fact that he looked like he'd showered and fixed his hair and his clothes were perfectly pressed. Had he secretly ironed when I went to bed? "It's not noon, is it?"

"No," he said quickly, "but you know me. I can't sleep the day away when there are things to do."

"You are aware this is a vacation, right? We aren't supposed to have a to-do list down here."

He harrumphed at this. "The best trips are perfectly planned, Annabelle. You know that."

"I'm as big a fan of schedules as the next wedding planner, but this is a vacation, not a trip. There's a difference. Besides, this celebration is supposed to be about what Kate likes, and the last thing she wants is to have a bachelorette party timeline."

He placed the bag on the wooden counter and started pulling out breads and pastries in various shapes and sizes. There were thin, sugar-crusted elephant ears, long strips of puff pastry, and puffy buns with deep grooves crisscrossing the tops.

I eyed them as I inhaled the distinctive scent of sugar. "Are these Mexican donuts?"

"They're pan dulce or Mexican sweet breads. I've had my chef attempt them for some parties, but they never taste the same as they do here."

"So Mexican donuts," I mumbled as I picked up one of the sticky elephant ears and took a bite. The flaky pastry crumbled in my mouth, but the burst of sugar made me moan with pleasure.

Richard arranged the remaining breads on a tray. "They're best fresh and they don't keep well, so I'll need to make a bread run in the mornings."

I dabbed at the crumbs clinging to my lips as I swallowed. "If it means more treats like this, I'll come with you tomorrow."

He walked back to the pool deck as Fern and Kate were peeling the paper masks from their faces. "Breakfast?"

Fern looked at the artfully arranged sweet breads and groaned. "The devil always takes such pleasing forms."

"Detox or no," Kate dropped her wet crumpled face mask on the side table and wiped her hands on the towel she was lying on, "this is my bachelorette celebration, so I'm going to surrender to the devil in all his delicious, sugary forms."

"When you put it that way." Fern wagged his eyebrows and plucked a sugar-crusted bun from the tray after Kate snagged one of the long pastries.

"Not as sugary as I expected," she said after she swallowed a bite.

"Which means we can eat more," Fern said through a mouthful.

Before we could all start in on seconds, there was a loud pounding from the front door.

Richard handed me the tray and spun around. "I hope Buster and Mack didn't lock themselves out. Where are they anyway?"

He stomped through the house to the front door and the rest of us followed behind. "You do know we're renting this home, and I'd like to return it to Gail in one piece—" he said as he threw open the door.

The two men standing at the front door were not Buster and Mack. They wore blue uniforms and looked a lot like police.

Fern squeaked and sank onto one of the white couches. "Not again."

"What do you mean not again?" I whispered.

"You know trouble follows us, Annabelle," Kate said.

"And dead bodies," Fern said in a low voice as his gaze darted around us.

"There are no dead bodies," I insisted, although now the fact that I hadn't seen Buster, Mack, or Leatrice this morning had me worried.

"English?" one of the men in uniform asked as he looked us over.

"*Si*," Richard answered. "We speak English."

"There was a report of dangerous men entering this house last night," the man said slowly. "Well, the call came in this morning, but it was about men entering last night."

Fern pressed a hand to his heart and flopped back on the cushion. "Are we victims of a home invasion and we didn't even know it?"

"Of course not," I said with more confidence than I felt. I had gone to bed before everyone had gotten back. Maybe someone else had left the doors unlocked.

"Who reported this?" Richard asked.

The other man glanced at a notebook. "The neighbor."

"Marla?" Richard and I both asked with so much disdain that the man looked up, startled.

"Yes, that is her name."

"What's going on?" Leatrice asked as she stumbled into the room in a pair of black footie pajamas with a life-sized, white skeleton printed on it.

Both officers gaped at her.

"Nothing," I said. "The neighbor we told you about reported seeing men breaking into our house."

"Terrifying criminals," one of the officers clarified, pronouncing the words carefully.

"There's been a break-in?" Buster asked as he and Mack walked up behind the two officers. They were both wearing pajamas identical to Leatrice's, although theirs were about twenty sizes bigger.

One of the men looked from Buster to Mack and dropped his notebook. "Dios mi! These are the criminals!"

CHAPTER 7

"What do you mean?" Mack pressed a hand to his heart and glanced behind him furtively, as if criminals might be lurking behind his considerable bulk. "Criminals? Where?"

Buster ran a hand over his bald head and folded his thick arms across his chest and the skeleton emblazoned on it. "I think he means us."

"Us?" Mack looked from Buster to the officers and then swung his gaze to all of us in turn. "They think we're criminals?"

The two officers exchanged uncomfortable looks and shifted on their feet. Finally, one cleared his throat. "The lady next door said she saw scary men dressed as skeletons entering this house last night."

Leatrice opened her mouth in outrage, then slid her gaze to our florist friends in skeleton pajamas. Her cheeks mottled pink. "Oh. Maybe the Halloween PJs weren't such a good idea."

"There's nothing wrong with their pajamas." Richard huffed out a breath and scowled. "The problem is the nosy neighbor who's more concerned with what's going on in our house than she ever was with what was happening in her own home."

The local officers appeared confused, but it was clear they sensed there was no crime to be investigated, and from the way they backed away, it was just as clear they didn't want to get involved with squabbles between tourists.

"I can see that there has been no break-in." One of the dark-haired men attempted to smile. "Sorry to bother you."

"You're not the one who should be sorry." Richard shot a deadly stare toward the house next door. "That woman is about to get a very unpleasant visit from me."

I put a hand on Richard's arm to calm him, darting a nervous look toward the officers. "He's not serious. We don't have any intention of causing trouble."

"Speak for yourself," Richard muttered darkly under his breath.

I gave a loud fake laugh as I followed the retreating officers out the open door, side-stepping a tiny green lizard that darted across the russet paving stones. "Thank you for stopping by."

After watching their patrol car drive away, I spun around and marched back inside. "What was that?"

Everyone was walking sleepily toward the kitchen, but they stopped and looked at me.

"I think those were police, Annabelle," Leatrice came up to me and gave me an indulgent smile.

I fought the urge to roll my eyes into the back of my head. "I know they were police." I pinned Richard with a sharp look. "What was with threatening our neighbor?"

Richard made a weak effort to appear offended. "You call that a threat? I was merely expressing my displeasure that Marla called the cops on us."

"I'm with Richard." Kate wiped crumbs from her mouth as she sank onto one of the couches. "That wasn't much of a threat coming from him."

Richard sniffed. "Thank you."

"He's threatened me with much more violence for asking him if his suit was off the rack."

Richard's smug expression faded, but he gave a loud sigh and flapped a hand in the air. "Why am I the one being attacked? It's Marla we should be united against."

Kate bobbed her head. "Again, I'm with Richard. If that woman thought there were men breaking into our house, why didn't she call us?"

Richard snapped his fingers and pointed at Kate. "I know she has the number since she and Gail are friends."

"Or even yell over?" Fern suggested from his reclined position on the couch. "It's not like we can't hear every word she says when she's outside on her pool deck or patio."

They had a point. If Marla had been so worried that we were being robbed or that our lives were in danger, why hadn't she raised more of an alarm than an after-the-fact call to the police? Then again, Marla didn't strike me as the kind of person who was so genuinely concerned about others as she was about herself. If she was worried about intruders, her interest most likely came from fear they could hit her home next. The other option was that she didn't think Buster and Mack were intruders at all and just wanted to cause trouble, although I wasn't sure why she'd do that. So far, we hadn't offended the woman. Or had we?

I followed Buster and Mack into the kitchen as they picked Mexican sweet breads to munch on and poured themselves steaming cups of coffee. "You didn't happen to meet our next-door neighbor, did you?"

Mack swallowed a bite of a crunchy, sugary pastry that sent bits of sugar cascading down the front of his pajamas. "You mean the bleached blonde who gives shrill a bad name?"

Unease tickled the back of my brain. "So you did meet her?"

"I wouldn't say that we met her." Leatrice padded into the kitchen behind me. "We ran into her when we were coming home last night."

"Almost literally." Buster's voice was even more gravelly than usual from sleep. "She was driving her Range Rover erratically and almost ran us off the road as she sped around our golf cart to drive into her own driveway."

"Then she yelled at Leatrice for being too old to be on the road." Mack circled an arm around the octogenarian's back.

"I think it was 'Get off the road, old lady.'" Buster added as he lifted his coffee mug to his lips.

Richard jerked around. "Leatrice was driving?"

"Don't tell me you two were drinking." I eyed my friends who were members of the Road Riders for Jesus and had given up their former hard-living ways, which I'd thought included heavy drinking.

"We weren't." Buster gave me a surreptitious wink. "But the roads were pretty deserted, and Leatrice said she'd never driven a golf cart."

"It doesn't handle as well as my Ford Fairmont, but you can't expect it to compete with a classic."

In no universe was Leatrice's mid-'80s model Ford a classic, but I just nodded. "I'm glad you weren't hurt, and I'm sorry she yelled at you."

Leatrice shrugged one bony shoulder. "That's okay, dear. Mack put her in her place."

I swiveled to my friend who was methodically rubbing one hand down his dark red goatee. "What did you say?"

Mack avoided my gaze. "I might have yelled back 'You first, honey.'" He released a heavy breath. "I know I should have turned the other cheek, but she was clearly in the wrong; she was driving horribly; and she almost caused an accident."

"I don't blame you," Fern said, winking at Leatrice. "I would have used a more colorful word than honey."

"That means she saw the three of you and saw you driving into our driveway." I frowned. It also meant there was a good chance Marla hadn't thought Buster and Mack were intruders. What were the chances that two enormous men would be staying in the house and also be trying to break into the house. With their distinctive bald heads, goatees, and overall size, you would have to be drunk or blind to mistake them for anyone else, even in the dark.

"See, Annabelle?" Richard sauntered into the kitchen and gave me a knowing look. "I was right to want to go over and give Marla a piece of my mind. I knew she was trouble from the moment she broke up the Bottinger marriage and fired me years ago, and she's still making trouble now."

"It wouldn't do any good to confront her," I said, even though my heart was racing from outrage at the woman. "She would only deny any malicious intent, and it would make us look bad to accuse her."

"Annabelle's right," Fern called from the couch. "Women like that never accept blame. It's better to find another way to exact our revenge."

Kate's eyes widened as she grinned. "Exacting revenge sounds fun."

"We are not going to be exacting revenge on anyone," I said, but my words were drowned out by the barrage of chatter.

"We could gather up all the lizards we can find and sneak them between the sheets of her bed." Leatrice rubbed her hands together. "Although I would hate for the lizards to be harmed."

"What about red dye in the pool?" Fern suggested.

"Change the lizards to frogs and we could have a solid plagues of Egypt theme," Mack said as he tapped one finger on his chin.

I held up both arms in the air. "No plagues of Egypt. No revenge. We're here for a fun getaway to celebrate Kate. We're not going to start a feud or get involved with anything that might get us in trouble, agreed?"

There were collective sighs, but everyone finally mumbled their agreement. I didn't like Marla, but there was no way I was going to let her spoil our fun—or our pool day.

CHAPTER 8

"Are we sure we want to be seen with criminals?" Fern teased as we gathered around the pool later that evening with cocktails in hand—or in my case, a fruity mocktail.

Leatrice wore a traditional Mexican dress covered in flowered embroidery, and Fern was in a black tuxedo with tails and a top hat. Buster and Mack had changed from their skeleton pajamas and were in a toned-down version of their usual biker attire—black jeans and leather vests with Road Riders for Jesus patches instead of the full leather pants and jackets.

Richard smoothed the front of his dark pants and cast a dark look at the house next to ours. "I think we all know that Marla knew exactly what she was doing when she reported us, but she's also the type to call the cops on a delivery guy because he doesn't look like he fits in the neighborhood."

Kate winked at Buster and Mack. "Or the bikers staying at a luxury villa."

"I'm surprised she didn't recognize you," Richard said. "Lush does the flowers for the top homes and events in the city. She must have crossed paths with you before."

Despite their unorthodox appearance—or maybe because of it— Lush, Buster and Mack's flower business and shop in Georgetown was sought after by even the snootiest DC socialites.

Buster made a face. "We did flowers for the first wife, who was a class act."

Richard nodded as if this explained everything. "Just like me. I think the second wife went out of her way to avoid using any of her predecessor's contacts."

"Fine by me," Mack said, scratching his goatee. "Especially if she thinks we look like criminals."

I was glad we could all laugh about it, but it had been a truly awkward few minutes to have to explain to the officers that the dangerous men Marla had reported were, in fact, guests at the house.

Luckily, Marla hadn't been out on her pool deck during the day, so we'd sunned and swam and indulged in sheet masks and drinks. It was only after we were thoroughly relaxed that we'd prepared to go into town for the official Day of the Dead parade and festivities.

"You don't have the look of criminals." Leatrice patted Mack on his beefy arm. "Trust me, hon. I spend a lot of time watching true crime shows, and you and Buster don't look a thing like real murderers and con men."

I didn't bother to remind Leatrice that we'd all encountered our fair share of killers over the years, and not all of them looked as scary and evil as you'd expect. I also wasn't sure if she remembered that our florist friends had been part of a tough motorcycle club before being born again and becoming Christian bikers, so who actually knew if they'd been involved in criminal activity. If they had, it was part of lives they'd left far in the past.

"I think it's great that someone thought you two were terrifying," Kate said, standing on tiptoes in her spike heels and throwing an arm around Buster's and Mack's shoulders. "That means that creepy guys won't bother us."

Richard sniffed and drew himself up. "Are you saying that Fern and I wouldn't act as proper deterrent to unwanted male attention?"

Fern smoothed the front of his shiny, red cummerbund and grinned at Kate. "If you don't want it, pass it over to me, sweetie."

Buster chuckled, the low rumble shaking his broad frame. "Reese already gave us strict orders to keep our eyes on the ladies."

Mack nodded. "Both Reese brothers."

"Isn't that sweet that they're looking out for us?" Leatrice fluttered her eyelashes, although I had a feeling my husband and Kate's fiancé hadn't been worried about our eighty-year-old neighbor being hit on by men.

I also doubted that my baby bump would attract much male attention—unless it was to send them scurrying away—but I loved that my husband still thought I could turn heads.

Fern raised his bright-green cocktail in the air. "Here's to a fun night out with our brave bodyguards—and Richard."

My best friend shot daggers at Fern. "The costume does not make you Zorro."

Fern's eyes nearly bugged out of his head. "I'm not Zorro. I'll have you know I'm a groom, one of the most popular symbols of the Día de los Muertos."

Never let it be said that Fern passed up the opportunity to immerse himself in other cultures, especially if that immersion included interesting fashion. I told myself that this costume was much more appropriate than the time he wore a kimono to do the hair for a Japanese wedding or a sari to our South Asian weddings.

"Cheers to Día de los Muertos!" Mack said loudly, tossing back his own drink, which I suspected might also be a mocktail.

We all took drinks, with Kate shuddering after she drained her glass. As she set her empty glass on a nearby table, she groaned. "Look who's also getting into the spirit of the holiday."

I followed her gaze to the pool deck next to ours and to the blonde in a wedding dress, a full face of skeleton makeup, and a circlet of red roses on top of her head.

"Cheese and crackers," Mack said under his breath since he and Buster didn't curse anymore. "Is that a real wedding dress?"

Fern squinted at the woman as she held a phone to her ear and stared off toward the water. "It doesn't look like a costume."

"It's not," Richard said with authority. "That's Badgley Mischka from about a decade ago. I'd bet my collection of Prada luggage on it."

"Ten years ago? Isn't that how long you said she's been married?" Kate put a hand to her mouth. "Is she wearing her own wedding dress to be a skeleton bride?"

As if she could sense we were talking about her, Marla swung her head around. Large, dark circles were painted to make her eyes look sunken, intricate swirls adorned her cheeks and forehead, and her mouth was painted to appear to be the teeth of a skull. The effect made us all gasp.

"Happy Día de los Muertos!" Fern called, waving one hand with vigor.

She nodded at us without cracking a smile then dropped the phone from her ear and spun around as a man strode toward her from inside.

Fern let out a low whistle. "I've gotten warmer receptions from actual corpses."

"That's our cue to leave," I said before Fern could launch into stories of doing hair for funerals.

I gave a final glance at Marla and the man, who I doubted was her employee considering how he was shaking his finger at her.

"They're sleeping together," Kate said to me as she flicked her gaze to the now arguing couple next door. Then Marla stomped away from him waving her arms. "At least they were."

"From what Carlita said, she's sleeping with every man on the island." Fern wrinkled his nose and inhaled quickly. "You don't think one of us is in danger of succumbing, do you?"

I glanced from him to Richard. "I think you're safe."

Richard mumbled something about hell freezing over as our group shuffled toward the door. "You don't think Marla knows her husband is on the island with future wife number three, do you?"

"You think that's why she's wearing her wedding dress and is painted like a skeleton?" I gave an involuntary shiver.

"That's one way to give your soon-to-be ex a fright." Richard shook his head. "And we thought we'd left DC drama behind us."

I hooked my arm through his. "As Kate would say, that's just wishful drinking."

CHAPTER 9

After parking our golf carts as close as we could to the small downtown area, our group made its way toward the graveyard where people were gathering for the parade. White stucco walls surrounded the raised graves, and the entrance was topped with a white cross that was stark against the oranges and golds of the setting sun. Music played gaily and residents were dressed up, with some in full traditional dress and faces painted.

"Do I smell churros?" Buster asked as the crowd parted for him and Mack, the smaller locals scurrying out of the way of the enormous men.

I inhaled the distinctive aroma of sugar and cinnamon. We'd seen churro stands around the town square the night before, and I had no doubt food stalls would be out in full force tonight. "I could go for a churro."

"I could go for a margarita," Kate said.

Before we could locate the source of the churro smell, a stocky woman in a ruffled skirt bustled up to Fern, looked him up and down, and spoke to him in rapid Spanish. He nodded and smiled as she pulled him away from us toward the front of the crowd gathering around the graveyard's entrance.

"What just happened?" Kate asked, as we watched Fern be propelled away from us and through the crowd.

Mack peered over the heads. "I think he might have become one of the parade leaders."

"That tracks," Richard muttered. "I told him his costumes were going to get him in trouble one day."

"Does he speak Spanish?" Kate asked me with a worried look toward the crush of people into which Fern had disappeared.

"Not enough to know what they're telling him."

Kate clutched my arm. "This is a harmless festival, right. They don't do any kind of sacrifices, do they?"

Richard rolled his eyes. "The ancient Maya stopped blood sacrifice to the gods hundreds of years ago. Besides, the Day of the Dead is about offerings of favorite food and drink to deceased relatives. Unless Fern was someone's favorite snack, he's safe."

"Fern does consider himself a snack," Kate said so only I could hear her, winking at me and giggling.

"Isn't this marvelous?" Leatrice rubbed her hands together as two women in heavily embroidered dresses and red flowers in their hair walked with a large blue banner between them that read "Festival de los Animas" and was embellished with skeletons in gold mariachi hats playing trumpets.

An almost eerie flute started to play as dusk fell, and candles were passed around. I put a hand on my belly and jumped up to try to get a glimpse of Fern, but as far as I could see, he was standing at the front of the procession flanked by enormous, costumed creatures in wildly colorful masks. The creatures were clearly men on stilts with extensions on their arms, so they appeared to have four long legs, but they were covered in painted feathers and their face masks made them look like fanged, fantastical beasts.

When I turned back to Leatrice, she had a red silk flower tucked into her jet-black hair.

She readjusted it. "What do you think?"

"You fit right in."

She beamed with pleasure, her eyes alight as the crowd began to move and the costumed creatures lurched forward. The flute music was slow and mournful, exactly the sounds I would associate with a cemetery, and a chill went down my spine.

Even though Fern was with the people walking behind the festival banner, the rest of us kept to the back. He was the only one who was dressed the part, anyway.

Richard clutched my arm. "Is that who I think it is?"

I followed his gaze, my own locking on the blonde in the wedding dress. She'd added a thick black face veil to her ensemble, but there was little question that it was Marla. She held a candle as she walked in the parade, but she wasn't walking straight.

"Is she drunk?" I asked.

"Hey," Kate said indignantly. "I'm not drunk. I would be if I could find a margarita around here though."

Richard made a face. "Not you. Her."

Kate followed his line of sight, her eyes widening when she spotted our neighbor. "She really came out in her old wedding dress, and apparently did a bit of pre-gaming first."

I couldn't see Marla's face through the lace of her face veil, but it didn't seem like she'd noticed us. Her head faced forward as she walked slowly, swaying slightly.

"Oh, look." Leatrice pointed at Marla. "Isn't that our neighbor? Yoo—"

The rest of her yoo-hoo was cut off by Richard grabbing her outstretched hand and clamping another hand over her mouth.

When he released her, she spluttered and wiped her mouth. "What was that for? I was only greeting our neighbor."

"Considering that she's already called the police on us once and hasn't seemed too thrilled by our presence next door, why don't we keep a low profile?" Richard said, wiping off his hand that was now stained with coral-pink lipstick.

"Low profile," Leatrice repeated. "I can do that. You might not remember, but I used to have quite a few costumes for my surveillance operations. If there's anyone who can blend in, it's me."

Richard's eyebrows popped up. Leatrice's wardrobe contained a significant number of footie pajamas, a Christmas tree skirt that actually lit up, and various themed outfits—all in a child's large or a ladies' ultra-petite. Despite her fondness for spy gear and monitoring the police scanner, she wasn't great at flying under the radar.

"Didn't she follow some of your neighbors in a trench coat and blonde wig until they moved out?" he whispered to me.

"Not all of them moved out. Some of them threatened to file a restraining order."

"Of course," Richard said. "My mistake."

"We don't need to worry about Marla seeing us," Kate said, nodding at the spot the woman had just occupied.

She was right. Marla was no longer in the parade, although I couldn't see where she'd gone even when I twisted my neck to peer up and down the street.

We were processing into an open square where a stage was set up in front of the Casa de Cultura with a brightly painted backdrop and folding chairs arranged in front. Strings of multicolored paper flags were hung overhead, and the costumed creatures ambled toward the stage as people filed into the chairs.

"I've found the churros," Mack said, pointing across the square to a portable food cart. "Who wants some?"

We all raised our hands.

Kate hooked her arms through Buster's and Mack's as they headed off toward the intoxicating scent of fried dough doused in cinnamon and sugar. "I'll go with you to help carry. Who knows? Maybe we'll find a margarita stand on the way."

"We can save seats." Leatrice walked purposefully toward the folding chairs that were quickly filling, and Richard and I followed.

"Now I know I'm not seeing things," Richard said, coming to a stop so abruptly that I walked into him.

"What now?" I asked.

He inclined his head toward a man with dark hair graying at the temples and a much younger blonde hanging on his arm.

I looked from the couple to Richard. "Is that…?"

"Mr. Bottinger," he said grimly. "Marla's ex-husband."

I swiveled my head to search for Marla, but she was nowhere to be seen. Had she seen her ex and left, or were we in for a showdown?

CHAPTER 10

"I think I ate too many churros." Mack patted his belly as we made our way back into the house. I couldn't tell if it was him or his leather vest that groaned as he moved.

"Is there such a thing as too many churros?" I asked, following him and gratefully sinking into the nearest chair.

We'd spent several hours at the festival watching the dance performances and cheering for the costume contest, but we'd also eaten plenty of hot, freshly deep-fried churros, which I'd decided might be my new favorite food.

"Not when you're eating for two." Kate flopped onto the white sofa across from me and kicked off her heels. How she'd managed in heels on the cobblestone and uneven pavement of downtown was beyond me. Then again, Kate's superpowers were being able to wear stilettos effortlessly and to determine if a couple was sleeping together at fifty paces. Shockingly, both of these had come in handy over the years.

I grinned at my former assistant and new business partner as a wave of exhaustion passed through me. She'd only managed to down a couple of margaritas, and I suspected this wasn't an accident. Even though Richard was the most outwardly protective of my pregnant state, it wasn't lost on me that Kate was keeping a more watchful eye on me. She didn't let me run around during our weddings and insisted I keep my feet up when we were taking breaks in the vendor room.

"Not that churros shouldn't be one of the major food groups, but who's up for a little late-night supper?" Buster asked as he puttered around the kitchen.

Kate and I both thrust our arms into the air.

"Count me in," Leatrice said, as she and Fern walked inside and closed the door behind them.

"Me too." Fern took off his top hat and smoothed a stray strand of dark hair. "I was too busy to eat a bite."

"What exactly was your role?" Kate patted the spot beside her, and Fern sat down.

"I couldn't tell you," he said. "I think I was roped into ceremonial duties since I was the only man dressed like a groom." He sniffed. "Or, I should say, the best dressed one."

Never let it be said that Fern was cursed with a lack of confidence.

"I still say I was robbed in the costume contest," he grumbled.

"You think you should have won over the child?" Buster asked from the kitchen as he and Mack pulled things from the refrigerator.

Fern looked affronted. "That child will have another chance next year. This may very well be my only Day of the Dead parade."

59

I reached over and patted his leg. "Tell you what. We'll throw our own Day of the Dead party next year and have a costume contest."

He brightened. "What a fabulous idea, sweetie. I can do a full face of skeleton makeup and really blow everyone out of the water."

"Our churros won't be as good," Kate said, "although I can make a pretty fierce margarita."

She was right that any churro we could replicate back in DC wouldn't taste as good as the ones in Mexico. There was something about being in a place surrounded by certain sights and sounds that made the food taste better.

Richard stomped into the house, and we all looked up. His face was flushed, and a lock of dark hair flopped uncharacteristically into his face.

"Where were you?" I'd thought he'd been right behind me when we came inside, and I'd assumed he'd slipped off to his room.

"I was parking the golf cart. Then I was accosted by crabs!"

"That sounds like a personal problem," Fern said behind his hand.

Richard glared at him. "No one told me that the island is overrun by nocturnal land crabs." He staggered to the only vacant chair and sank into it. "I was nearly eaten alive."

I exchanged a glance with Kate. We were no strangers to Richard's tendency to overdramatize things, but flesh-eating crabs were a first.

"Where are these carnivorous crabs?" Kate asked.

Richard flapped a hand in the direction of the front door. "The patio and driveway are crawling with them. See for yourself."

Kate and I both stood, too tempted by Richard's description to miss the chance to see if the house was truly being invaded by crabs. Leatrice hurried along behind us murmuring about how exciting it was.

I opened the heavy, wooden door expecting to see an empty gravel drive. Instead, I almost shrieked as I jumped back. Richard hadn't been lying. The driveway was covered with large hard-shelled crabs almost a foot wide that were slowly moving sideways on spindly legs.

"There must be a hundred of them," Kate gasped.

"Chips and salsa!" Mack said from behind us, his mouth hanging open and his oven-mitted hands pressed to both sides of his cheeks. I guessed this clean curse was a regional update to his usual 'cheese and crackers.'

"For the love of everything holy," Richard cried from the great room, "don't let them in. I barely outran them!"

Although they weren't small, they also weren't moving quickly. Still, they didn't seem dissuaded by our appearance at the doorway, and they didn't scuttle away from us or the light spilling outside.

I leaned against the door until it slid shut, giving an involuntary shudder that so many spider-looking creatures were amassed outside our rental house. "I'm guessing your friend Gail didn't mention the giant crabs when she told you about the house?"

Richard fanned himself with one hand as he lay sprawled on the chair. "She did not."

"Does anyone else have a sudden craving for crab cakes?" Fern asked.

"We can offer you quesadillas," Buster said from the kitchen, an apron wrapped around his leather vest.

"They're cooking?" Richard asked me in a stage whisper. "Do they cook?"

As DC's most illustrious caterer, Richard forgot that other people knew how to function in kitchens. Since I wasn't much of a cook, I hadn't done much to change his assumption that everyone was suffering from subpar culinary skills until he came on the scene.

"If anyone doesn't want quesadillas, I could always make my taco salad," Leatrice said. "Do we have raisins?"

"Raisins?" Richard said the word like it was a curse, leapt to his feet, and hurried toward the kitchen. "Bite your tongue."

Before I could see how the triumvirate in the kitchen would work, my phone vibrated in my pocket. I pulled it out and smiled when I saw my husband's name on the screen. As Richard's voice rose as he started to issue commands to his newly deputized sous chefs, I pushed myself to my feet and padded toward the sliding glass door. "I'm going to take this outside."

Kate gave me a thumbs up, and Fern told me to tell my hunky husband hello.

"Hey, babe." Mike's deep voice was like a balm as I left the squawking of the house behind and walked further onto the pool deck. The moon was high in the midnight-blue sky, and the opalescent light bounced off the sea and the smooth surface of the pool.

I was glad that no crabs could climb the wall surrounding the pool deck, although I could still see over the white stucco to the house next door, and I noted that Marla's lights were blazing.

"Hey yourself." It had only been a little over twenty-four hours since we'd spoken, but it felt like forever.

"How are you feeling? Are you getting enough rest? Did Richard take care of your bags? I made him swear on his wardrobe that he wouldn't let you carry anything."

I laughed. "Your threats worked. He insisted on dragging both of our suitcases and taking my carry-on, which was a little painful to watch. You do know I'm not injured, right?"

"I know you always push yourself too hard. Being pregnant is one of the few times when you can take it easy and get Richard to do manual labor. Milk it while you can, babe."

I laughed again. "That's true. Usually I'm the pack mule."

"Aside from Richard being your beleaguered porter, how is Mexico?"

"It's nice. The island is small, which is great. The house has a beautiful view, and it's private." I glanced at a figure emerging from Marla's house, instantly recognizing the wedding gown and face veil. "For the most part."

Before I could wave to her, she turned and went back into her house as silently as she'd walked from it. Should I mention the weird situation with Marla and her ex, or would the gossip just bore my husband?

I decided to instead tell him about the festival we'd attended and all the churros we'd eaten, which made him laugh. "I'd better get back inside," I finally told him as I peered through the sliding doors and saw Richard with his hands on his hips and one foot tapping on the floor. "Richard took over cooking, and I'm not sure how it's going."

After exchanging some tender "I love yous," I hung up and pivoted back to the house.

"Don't you dare walk away from me!"

Even though the scream came from next door and was muffled slightly by the fact that it emerged from inside Marla's house, I almost jumped out of my own skin. I squinted hard to see who Marla was yelling at but could only make out a male figure walking briskly past several windows on the side of the house before a car's motor revved up, and it peeled from the pebbled driveway. Was it the man we'd seen with her earlier?

Marla's life was definitely not dull, although I wished it were a bit quieter.

CHAPTER 11

"Top of the morning!"

I rubbed my eyes as I emerged from my bedroom and followed the sound of the overly cheery greeting. Was I hallucinating, or was Fern in the kitchen wearing an apron and a chef's hat?

"What's happening?" I pulled my hair into a pony-tail as I shuffled across the great room and eyed the hairdresser standing behind the wood-topped island with a knife in his hand.

He waved the knife as if him cooking was the most normal thing in the world. "It's morning, and I'm making breakfast."

I glanced out the sliding glass doors to where the sun was peeking over the horizon, the warm gold rays making the blue water glitter like it was studded with diamonds. It was so bright it made me squint. "But you never wake up this early, and you don't cook."

"Au contraire, sweetie." Fern grinned at me, his puffy white chef's hat tilted rakishly to one side. "I can cook; I just usually choose not to."

I opened the sliding glass door and breathed in the fresh morning air, stepping outside long enough to hear our neighbor shrieking at someone.

She was getting an early start, I thought, as I walked onto the pool deck and picked up an empty glass from the day before. Dew covered the lounge chairs, and Marla's voice was the only thing puncturing the perfect morning calm. After a brief glance toward her house, where I could see her pacing silhouette through her own glass doors, I made my way back inside, wondering why she'd decided to stay in her wedding dress. Had she passed out in it?

I pushed thoughts of the brash blonde from my mind and returned my attention to Fern. I slid onto one of the stools on the other side of the kitchen island. "I assumed you'd be sleeping in after last night."

"Last night?" He laughed. "We're up later than that most wedding days."

He had a point. Our wedding days were usually long with load-out not completed until the wee hours of the mornings or sometimes almost dawn. As the hairdresser, Fern didn't need to stay until every vendor was loaded from the venue, but he did insist on staying through the reception in case the bride needed touch-ups—giving her "the full Fern," as he called it—and almost always ended up joining us for late-night supper at one of our Georgetown haunts.

"You're right about that." I yawned. "I guess the pregnancy has made me crave sleep because I could easily go another eight hours."

"And miss this glorious day?" Fern swept wide the arm not holding the knife. "The island might be small, but there's still so much we haven't seen and done. There's the lighthouse and the graveyard overlooking the sea."

I nodded, remembering passing the cemetery on our way to and from the house. Like the one downtown, the graveyard was filled with raised tombs adorned with colorful crosses and statuary. "Since when do you know so much about the island?"

"The ladies at the parade were telling me all about it. They were giving me lots of tips about what we should see and do while we're here. They also told me how to make huevos rancheros, which is what I'm doing now."

"Huevos rancheros?"

Fern dropped a corn tortilla into a frying pan, and it sizzled. "They said this is a classic Mexican breakfast dish." He poked at the frying tortilla with a wooden spoon. "It's got fried tortillas, salsa, beans, cheese, and eggs. What could be better than that?"

"Sounds delicious," Leatrice said as she joined us in her skeleton footie pajamas.

"Sounds like a heart attack," Richard mumbled as he emerged from the other side of the house.

"Nonsense." Fern brushed off Richard's comment with a wave of his spoon, sending drops of oil across the kitchen. "The people here eat this all the time."

"And have you seen how many graveyards there are for an island this size?" Richard whispered as he took the stool next to me.

I elbowed him in the ribs. "I think it amazing that Fern's making us an authentic Mexican breakfast."

"One thing that's not going to be traditionally Mexican are the Bloody Marys." Fern motioned his head to a bottle of tequila behind him on the counter. "Who wants to start mixing up a batch?"

"Me!" Leatrice rubbed her hands together as she bounced over to the counter behind Fern. "I've always wanted to be a bartender."

"It's never too late to pursue a dream," Fern told her solemnly, twisting around to pin her with an intense gaze. "Don't let anyone tell you that you can't embrace those crazy passions."

Richard sucked in a breath. "Are you out of your mind?"

"What?" Fern gave him a look of innocence. "I think our old girl would make a fabulous bartender."

"Not that," Richard said with a frown. "You can't make Bloody Marys with tequila."

Fern shrugged. "It's the only booze we have unless someone wants to take a trip downtown to hunt down vodka, although I doubt the shops are open. This doesn't seem like an island that rouses early."

I pressed my lips together to suppress a wave of nausea at the thought. "Tequila in the morning? You'll never make it until nighttime before passing out."

Fern winked at me. "Making it until nighttime is not my goal, sweetie. It's making it to the pool deck for an after-breakfast siesta."

Fern flipped some of his fried tortillas over and added some more to the pan. The smell of the frying corn reminded me that I hadn't had a bite to eat since the quesadillas last night, but I'd only had a few bites since I'd lingered on the patio longer than I should, and most of the food had been gone by the time I'd come inside. At the time I hadn't been too concerned since I'd been distracted by the scene next door, but now my stomach growled in protest.

"I wouldn't mind a virgin Bloody Mary," I called out to Leatrice. "Extra celery and light on the spice."

Richard cut me a side-eye glance. "So, tomato juice with a celery stalk?"

"Blasphemy," Buster said in a low rumble as he and Mack walked in through the front door.

I jumped a bit, forgetting for a beat that they were sleeping in the attached guesthouse, which had a separate entrance and wasn't connected directly to the main house.

Mack shook his head and jerked a thumb at Buster. "This one puts hot sauce on everything. He's never met a Bloody Mary that's spicy enough."

"Make that three virgin Bloodys," Buster said, "but make mine extra spicy."

Leatrice bobbed her head as she started to assemble her ingredients on the counter, pushing the bottle of tequila behind the containers of tomato juice.

"Bloody Marys?" Kate stumbled from her bedroom and pushed a pink satin eye mask to the top of her head. "I thought we were in Mexico, people. What about Tequila Sunrise Mimosas?"

"I'm just trying to get some nutrition," I said as she took the stool Leatrice had vacated next to me at the island.

"A Tequila Sunrise Mimosa has a wedge of orange for a garnish." Kate flicked her fingers through her tousled blonde hair.

"That should fill me up," I deadpanned.

Fern slid the fried tortilla onto a plate and scooped some pico de gallo on the side. "Breakfast should be ready momentarily. You can't rush haute cuisine."

"Or chips and salsa," Richard said as he raised an eyebrow and watched Fern cook.

Fern shot him a murderous look but was prevented from responding with a snappy retort by Leatrice bustling over to me with a tall glass filled with tomato juice and what appeared to be an entire stalk of celery taking up half the glass.

"Give this a sip, hon."

I smiled at her as I lifted the glass to my lips, holding the celery with my other hand so it wouldn't hit me in the face. I took a small sip. "Tomato juice."

"You did say light spice," Leatrice beamed at me, "so I stuck with tomato juice."

I took another drink. There was nothing wrong with tomato juice. "Thanks, Leatrice. It's perfect."

Kate slipped off her stool. "I'll start on the Tequila Sunrise Mimosas." She glanced back at me. "I'll make yours virgin."

"So, just orange juice?"

She gave me a wicked smile. "To go with your tomato juice."

Fern held an egg in each hand over a second, smaller fry pan. "And now for the fried eggs."

A bloodcurdling scream made us all turn toward the door as Carlita ran inside, her eyes wild and leaves sticking out of her dark hair.

"Shiitake mushrooms!" Mack cried, staggering back as the woman hurried toward us frantically.

Richard pressed a hand to his heart. "What on earth?"

"It's Marla," Carlita said between gasps. "She's dead!"

We all froze, the room going quiet except for the crunch of cracking eggshells. I turned to see Fern wide-eyed as raw egg ran through his fingers.

CHAPTER 12

"Breakfast is ruined," Fern wailed as the eggs glopped partly into the pan and partly onto the stove.

"Of course," Richard muttered to himself as he cradled his head in his hands. "How could I expect us *not* to encounter a dead body?"

Leatrice bounced up and down on her toes, a stalk of celery in one hand. "She is?"

Carlita stared at us then gave her head a small shake as if she couldn't quite believe what she was seeing. "Did you hear what I said?"

Fern sighed. "We heard." He tossed the eggshells into the trash. "This isn't our first rodeo."

"Rodeo?" Carlita wrinkled her nose in confusion.

"It's not the first time we've encountered a dead body before," I explained, sliding from my stool. Aside from the screaming, I was a bit startled that she thought Marla was dead when I'd seen her and heard her not half an hour earlier. Maybe she'd been mistaken, and the woman was passed out or sleeping.

"Technically we haven't encountered it," Buster said, nodding to the distressed woman who looked like she wasn't sure if she'd run from the frying pan into the fire. "She did."

I took Carlita's hands and led her to the couch. "Why don't you tell me what happened?"

She sank onto the white cushion, her shoulders deflating and her gaze dropping. "It was horrible. I came in to clean and there she was." She waved a hand at some imaginary object on the floor. "Dead."

Kate joined us on the couch with a glass in hand. It was filled with orange juice that I suspected with spiked with tequila, at the very least. "You're sure she's dead?"

Carlita nodded without looking up. "I could tell right away. Her skin looked wrong, but I shook her to be sure." She shivered. "And she was cool to the touch."

Kate winced. "You touched her?"

"Only to be sure." Carlita shook her head. "But I knew before I felt for her pulse."

I knew what she meant. Dead bodies looked different, and there was an instinctive part of us that knew before our fears were confirmed. But if Carlita was right, then Marla had died only minutes ago. Another shiver slithered down my spine. Had the women died while we'd been sitting in the kitchen laughing about Bloody Marys? And what had killed her? She didn't seem old enough to have had a heart attack.

I patted the woman's shoulder, deciding not to pepper her with the questions flooding my mind. She wasn't in any state to answer them, even if she did know anything beyond what she'd told us. I didn't know Carlita well, but I felt for her. She'd clearly had a shock, one I'd personally experienced more times than I'd like to admit.

"What did you do after you made sure she was dead?" I asked.

Carlita glanced up at me, gnawing the corner of her lip nervously. "I panicked when I realized that she was actually dead. That's when I ran from the house and came over here as fast as I could."

"Did you call the police?" Kate asked, her voice gentle.

Carlita shook her head, her brow furrowing. "I didn't even think about it. I was too terrified."

Seeing a dead body for the first time was shocking, and a small shudder went through me as I remembered the first body I'd tripped over—literally. If I closed my eyes, I could still recall the waxy, blue face mottled with various colors from the reflection of the stained glass. I gave myself a shake to dislodge the bad memories and return my focus to the dead body at hand.

"Don't worry," I reassured her. "We can call the authorities for you."

She made a face. "I know the policia on the island. I don't know if they can handle this. They might need to bring in officers from Cancun."

"You don't have deaths on Isla?" Kate asked.

"That would be odd, considering the festival we attended last night," Richard said as he walked over to us. "Not to mention the multiple graveyards that take up prime real estate."

Carlita looked at us like we were crazy. "Of course, people die here, but we almost never have murders."

Richard's knees buckled, and he sank like a stone into a nearby chair. "Did you say murder?"

"Yes, murder." She fanned her face. "Why do you think I'm so upset?"

I exchanged a glance with Kate, slightly abashed that I'd assumed the woman was hysterical because she'd encountered a corpse. "You didn't say she was murdered when you came in. You said she was dead."

"It wasn't natural causes?" Leatrice bustled over holding a pair of blood-red drinks garnished with celery stalks the size of saplings. She shoved one at Carlita and started drinking the other one. "Here, dear, you probably need this more than the rest of them."

Carlita eyed the frilly leaves of the celery bursting from the top of the glass. "Gracias."

Leatrice perched on the other side of the woman and patted her leg. "Why are you sure it's murder?"

"Probably the knife sticking from her back."

Kate almost choked on her drink, while Richard slumped deeper into his chair with a squeak.

"She was stabbed in the back?" Fear iced my skin. "But I saw her pacing inside her house and talking on the phone not too long ago."

Fern jerked his head up as he crushed another egg in his hand. "What?" Then he scowled as more egg goo oozed between his fingers.

"When I went outside this morning, I distinctly saw Marla inside her house in her wedding dress."

Carlita bobbed her head up and down. "She was wearing her wedding dress when I found her."

"That wasn't more than half an hour ago," Fern said, seemingly frozen in place as the egg dripped onto the stovetop again.

Buster widened his stance as he glanced toward the front door and then the sliding glass one leading to the patio. "Which means the killer might still be nearby."

"That's it." Richard leapt to his feet and pulled his phone from his pajama bottoms. "I'm booking us the first flights out. Someone has taken the Day of the Dead too far."

"Tourists ruin everything," Kate said with a thoughtful shake of her head.

"You know what this really means?" Leatrice leaned over Carlita, her eyes sparkling with delight. "We might be able to catch the killer before they escape."

Carlita looked from me to Leatrice. "I'm not sure if I came to the right place."

"You and me both, sister," Richard said under his breath as he tapped at his phone screen. "You and me both."

CHAPTER 13

"You aren't serious?" Richard stared at me as I stood. "About the killer being nearby?" I swept my gaze toward the back of the house and the glass doors that overlooked the water. "If Marla was killed in the past half an hour, and the killer isn't in the house, then they escaped to the road or to the beach."

My well-honed wedding planner instinct to solve problems kicked into high gear as I assessed all the possibilities. We'd encountered enough murders that I didn't react with shock and hysteria anymore, but I did have the need to fix things, and a killer on the loose during Kate's bachelorette celebration was a problem that needed solving.

"What if they dove into the sea?" Fern's eyes were wide as he walked from the kitchen, wiping his hands on a dish towel. "They could have had diving equipment waiting for them at the bottom of the rocks and gone into the water without a trace."

Kate tilted her head to one side as she took a sip of her drink. "That's dramatic."

"And premeditated," I said. "We don't know if this was a planned murder or a crime of passion."

Leatrice rubbed her hands together almost gleefully. "I love crimes of passion."

Carlita's head ping-ponged between all of us, her look of confusion deepening.

Richard held up his hands. "Whatever it was, *we* aren't involved with it." He pinned me with a fierce gaze. "I promised your other half that I would keep you safe and make sure you didn't get into any trouble." He flapped a hand at my baby bump. "I thought that wouldn't be a huge undertaking considering the fact that you're pregnant and fall asleep by eight o'clock."

I bristled slightly at this. "It's not always eight."

He narrowed his eyes at me. "Not the point, darling."

"We're not getting involved," I said, taking Carlita's hand. "We're merely calling the authorities and preserving the crime scene until they arrive."

Richard folded his arms across his chest. "And have we called the authorities?"

I opened my mouth and closed it. "Not yet." I didn't want to admit that I had no idea how to summon help on the Mexican island. Dialing 9-1-1 would get me nowhere fast.

Kate produced her phone from a mysterious pocket in her shortie PJs. "I'll make the call." She turned to Carlita. "How do I call the policia?"

"Do you speak any Spanish?" Richard asked.

She gave him a mischievous smile. "I've dated my share of hot Latino men, so I know enough to get by."

"You've probably dated my share too," Richard mumbled, earning him a snarky look from Kate as Carlita gave her a number to call.

"Since that's taken care of, we should secure the crime scene," I said in a low voice as Kate spoke in broken Spanish to someone on the other end of the phone.

"Don't even think about it." Richard shook a finger at me so hard I was afraid it might fly off. "You're in no condition to be traipsing around a crime scene."

"Do I need to remind you again that I'm not an incapacitated?"

"And do I need to remind you that your husband is a cop who carries a gun and will not be happy if he hears I let you get mixed up in a murder in another foreign country?"

Leatrice clapped her hands together. "This would make the third foreign country in which you've gotten involved in a murder investigation." She tapped a wrinkled finger on her chin. "Maybe I should get you one of those scratch-off maps you can hang on the wall."

Fern snapped his fingers and nodded. "There's an idea for nursery decor!"

"No," Richard and I said in unison, making Fern jump and blink rapidly, muttering something about out-of-the-box thinking never getting its proper due.

I couldn't help grinning at Richard. We might not agree on everything, but he still had my back. I blew out a long breath. "I completely understand your concern, but I'm not suggesting I go over there alone."

He put a hand to his throat. "Me?"

"We'll go." Buster lumbered over and adjusted the motorcycle goggles on top of his smooth head. "If the killer is still anywhere in sight, we should be able to scare him off."

Mack joined him, the two of them side by side creating a human wall that would have been even more intimidating if they hadn't been in skeleton pajamas. Even so, they were massive men who looked like they belonged in a motorcycle club that *didn't* hold prayer meetings and Bible study.

"Happy?" I asked Richard. I was itching to go next door and see if what Carlita had told us was true. I had a hard time reconciling the fact that I'd just seen the woman alive and well and talking loudly with someone on her phone. Since eyewitnesses were notoriously bad at recalling detail—especially under duress—I wanted to see for myself that Marla had actually been killed. I hadn't found her to be the most pleasant woman, but who on the island had hated her enough to want her dead?

Richard's perfectly arched brows rose. "Am I happy that the house my friend Gail gifted us for a few days is coincidentally next door to a crime scene?" He tapped one foot rapidly on the floor. "What do you think?"

"I don't think he is," Fern said in a stage whisper.

"Then come with us." I motioned for him with one arm as I walked toward the door with Buster and Mack. Leatrice fell in step with us. I gave her a quick glance before realizing it would be pointless to tell her to stay behind. My neighbor had been known to crash my weddings and use listening devices to stay in the know. I only wished she wasn't also wearing skeleton pajamas that matched Buster and Mack. We looked like a strange gang with two burly enforcers and an eighty-year-old whose snug-fitting, skeleton pajamas bloused around her knees.

"I'll stay here with Carlita." Kate tucked her phone away and patted the woman on the knee. "The police will be at the house soon."

"And I'll stay and finish making breakfast." Fern cast a mournful look at the kitchen. "If we have any more eggs."

"We'll be back soon," I said. "Once the police arrive, I'm sure they'll take over, and we'll be out of it."

Richard made a scoffing sound in the back of his throat. "If I had a dollar…"

I ignored his complaints as he trudged with us from the house and across the makeshift path between the two properties. The crabs that had covered the pebbled driveway the night before were gone, although it was clear by the patterns in the pale gray stones that they'd been scuttling around all night.

I pushed aside a palm frond that blocked the path through the greenery, held it for Leatrice, and then followed Buster and Mack to the front door of Marla's house. Like the house we were using, the outside was white stucco, but instead of a thatched roof, this house was all sharp, modern angles.

The glossy, black door hung open. No doubt, Carlita had run outside so fast she hadn't bothered to close it behind her.

"Let's remember not to touch anything," I said, instinctively dropping my voice. I knew we shouldn't be entering the crime scene in the first place, but the least we could do was to avoid damaging any evidence.

Buster nudged the front door open the rest of the way without touching the door handle, and we all walked behind him single file. Within a few steps inside the house, I was hit with the pungent, coppery smell of blood. I raised a hand to my nose and suppressed the urge to heave. Pregnancy had made my sense of smell as acute as a bomb-sniffing dog, but I was surprised that the scent of blood was so strong when the murder was so fresh.

The entrance opened onto one massive room, much like our house, with a floor-to-ceiling glass wall fronting the Caribbean. The furnishings were as stark as the exterior of the home with lots of chrome and gray and almost no indication that the house was in Mexico. Half-filled cocktail glasses sat on the glass side tables and coffee table, the contents watery. Before I could comment on the lack of personality in the home, Buster and Mack both stopped short.

I peered around them to the sunken living room and the body lying sprawled on the floor. But it was the man standing over it with bloody hands that made me gasp.

CHAPTER 14

"Mr. Bottinger?" Richard's voice from behind startled me.

I whirled to him, then whipped my head back to study the man standing over the body more closely. Richard was right. It was the man with dark hair graying at the temples that we'd seen last night at the festival. The only difference was that now the young blonde that had been hanging on his arm was gone, and his hands were dripping with blood.

He twisted at the sound of Richard saying his name, and his mouth hung open. "Richard Gerard?"

"What are you doing here?" Richard asked, his voice remarkably calm.

"I...we..." the man glanced down at the body and winced, "we were supposed to meet to talk about the house."

Buster and Mack walked closer, but I sidled around them so I could get a better view of the body. As Carlita had described, the blonde lay face down with a knife protruding from her back, but I couldn't be sure it was Marla until I'd edged my way around to glimpse the side of her face that tilted up. I flinched when I recognized the woman's features.

If the distinctive wedding dress and blonde hair hadn't been proof enough, seeing her face convinced me that the body was Marla. I swallowed hard, the scent of blood even more powerful the closer I walked.

"Oh, dear," Leatrice said.

I jumped when I realized she was standing right next to me. When she wasn't wearing clothes with bells, she could be surprisingly stealthy.

I pivoted back to the body. It was obvious that Carlita had been right about it being murder since what appeared to be a kitchen knife protruded from her back. Curiously, there was a pool of blood underneath her that had soaked into the white carpet covering the sunken part of the room. I didn't want to move the body or even get much closer to it, but I wondered if she'd been stabbed in her chest or stomach as well. It would explain the amount of blood that had amassed in such a short time.

"Did you and Marla fight?" Richard asked, scooting closer to me and grabbing my arm.

"Fight?" Mr. Bottinger sounded dazed as he looked down at his own hands and droplets of blood dripped onto the floor. Then he jerked his head up. "You think I did this?"

Buster, Mack, Richard, and I all exchanged looks as Leatrice edged closer to the body, muttering to herself.

"You are standing over your ex-wife's body," Richard said, motioning with a flick of his fingers to the man's own hands, "with literal blood on your hands."

"We know you and Marla were in a nasty divorce battle over the house," I said. "She told us that you were trying to force her from it."

He shook his head. "Not like this. I would never have hurt her, even if she was making my life a living hell." He laughed dryly. "With Marla, that was par for the course."

"Who else would want her dead if not you?" I pressed. "Did she know your new girlfriend is on the island with you?"

He let out another mirthless laugh. "Of course, she knew. Marla knew everything, and she forgot nothing, which means she remembered when she was here with me as the new girlfriend."

That tracked with what Richard had heard from his friend Gail, but it didn't make Mr. Bottinger seem any less guilty.

"But the only person who benefits from your ex-wife's death is you, right?" I asked. "With her gone, there's no battle over the vacation home or half of your estate."

His brow wrinkled as he shook his head. "She never would have gotten half. We had a prenup, which is why she never would have gotten this house, either. As soon as our divorce was settled, the house would have reverted to me." He glanced down at the body and grimaced. "I had no reason to kill her."

There were plenty of reasons for ex-husbands—or soon-to-be ex-husbands—to want to kill their wives, and I wasn't convinced that Mr. Bottinger didn't have some. I'd known Marla barely two days, and I could have coughed up one or two reasons to want the woman dead.

A commotion at the door made us all turn toward the uniformed police rushing in. They wore navy blue from head to toe and had metallic star-shaped badges flashing on their chests.

When they spotted Mr. Bottinger standing over the body, they stopped and started yelling in Spanish.

Marla's soon-to-be ex raised his bloody hands over his head as the police rushed toward him, and I cringed as they walked around the body, even bumping it as they jerked his hands behind his back. Leatrice, who'd been kneeling near Marla, stood quickly and scurried back to stand by me.

"I'm innocent," he cried as he was roughly handcuffed. "I didn't kill her!"

His pleas were ignored as he was pulled from the room, and we stepped back to allow him to pass.

When he reached Richard, Mr. Bottinger leaned toward him. "You have to help me. You know me. You've worked for me. You know I'm not a killer."

Richard opened and closed his mouth.

Mr. Bottinger struggled as he was yanked forward. "I've heard about the murder cases you've helped solve. You have to help me, Richard." His voice cracked as he was dragged away, but he raised it to a scream. "I swear I'm innocent!"

A chill went through me at the desperation in his voice. Either he was innocent, or he was an excellent actor.

After Mr. Bottinger was led away, we were unceremoniously ushered out of the house, as well. A female officer did take our names, our statements, and the information that we'd seen multiple other men at the house but didn't have any idea of their names and had made note that we were staying next door.

An officer with a thick mustache barked something at us in Spanish as he strode past us into return to the house and murder scene.

The female officer translated for us. "Do not leave the island without speaking to us first. We will be in contact for additional statements after we have processed the crime scene."

Buster and Mack led us back toward our house in silence. When we reached the front door, Mack released a breath. "I still can't believe we actually walked in on the killer."

Buster shook his head. "I can't believe we can't leave the island."

"Leave the island?" Richard huffed out a breath. "Why would we leave when we have a murder to solve and an innocent man to clear?"

I gaped as he strode into the house. "Wait, what happened to staying out of trouble?"

Richard looked at me like I'd taken leave of my senses. "Never let it be said that Richard Gerard abandoned a client with the potential to throw numerous elaborate parties in his time of need."

CHAPTER 15

"What do you mean Marla's ex-husband was there?" Kate asked as she sat at the kitchen island and sipped a fresh drink, this one with a splash of red in the orange juice.

Leatrice nodded. "Standing over the body with blood on his hands."

Fern shuddered as he slid some fried eggs onto Kate's plate, and they landed on top of the crispy tortilla topped with refried beans. "That's not a pretty picture."

Carlita still sat on the couch, her gaze darting to Richard when he revealed that we'd encountered Mr. Bottinger at the murder scene. "There was no one else in the house when I found her." Then her eyebrows pressed together. "At least, I didn't think there was."

Richard pointed at the woman. "That proves that my client was right when he said he was innocent."

"Your client?" I didn't make any attempt to hide my shock. "You haven't worked for the man since he divorced his first wife. Don't tell me you're falling for his ploy."

"Ploy?" Richard gave an affronted sniff. "I hardly think an innocent man protesting his wrongful arrest is a ploy."

"How do you know he's innocent?" Buster asked. "From what I saw, he had motive and opportunity."

Richard frowned. "Carlita walked in on the body. Mr. Bottinger wasn't there. He obviously showed up after Carlita came to tell us and before we walked over."

"Unless he killed Marla, heard Carlita coming and hid, then came back when she'd gone," Mack suggested as he walked to the kitchen and took the plate of food Fern handed him.

Richard braced a hand on his hip. "Why would he come back to the body after he'd killed her—assuming he killed her, which he didn't?"

I shrugged. "Maybe he was trying to get the murder weapon so he could hide it or wipe the prints."

"Then why were his hands covered in blood?" Richard tapped one toe on the floor in rapid-fire. "If he stabbed her, he wouldn't have gotten his hands bloody. The only way you'd do that is if you were trying to save her or roll her over."

He had a point. The person who'd plunged the knife into her back wouldn't have had any reason to touch the pool of blood beneath her body.

"Let me get this straight." Fern held up his wooden serving spoon as he paused in doling out breakfast. "The woman's ex-husband, who she was in a nasty divorce battle with, was at the house they were fighting over? She's dead and he's covered in her blood, and you think he shouldn't be suspect numero uno?"

Richard pressed his lips together.

"Aren't we forgetting the guy she was fighting with last night?" Kate asked.

"Exactly." Richard snapped his fingers and pointed to Kate. "We all saw that lovers' spat, and it wasn't with her ex."

I remembered the shadowy male figure I'd seen last night, but I couldn't have told you who that had been. I did know that they'd driven away from the house.

"I think it's very interesting that you're suddenly fine with us getting involved with the case, but you weren't a few minutes ago." I hopped onto the bar stool beside Kate. "What happened to safety being the priority, and my husband objecting to me being sucked into another murder investigation?"

"I never said *you* should get involved," Richard said.

"This should go over well," Fern said in a low voice as he swiveled his head between me and my best friend.

"Your plan is to solve the crime and clear Mr. Bottinger without my help?" I took the glass of straight orange juice that Kate handed me wordlessly.

"That's the story I'm telling your husband. He's already going to be upset that someone was killed in the house next door to ours. If I tell him I stood by while you got embroiled in an investigation, there's no chance of the baby being named Gerard."

Kate held a hand to her mouth and talked from one side. "Was that even a possibility?"

I shook my head just enough for Kate to notice.

"I'm the one who was asked to help," Richard continued. "There's no reason for anyone else to be pulled into this."

"But we all have to stay on the island," Mack said. "It's not like we can leave until we're questioned."

Buster swallowed a mouthful. "They might have taken the ex-husband away, but the police didn't seem happy that we were at the crime scene."

"They'll want to talk to you, too," I told Carlita, who nodded mutely.

"You're sure you don't want any huevos rancheros?" Fern asked with a wave of his spoon, sending a glob of refried beans sailing across the kitchen.

She shook her head and stood, with a suspicious glance at Fern's attempt at a Mexican breakfast. "I should be getting home since I won't be cleaning Marla's house." Then she paused. "Do you need me to clean here?"

"Don't be silly." Mack put an arm around her shoulder and walked her to the door. "You've had a terrible shock. You should go home and rest. We're big kids. We can clean up after ourselves."

I eyed the kitchen, which appeared to have been turned inside out. Fern might know how to cook, but I wasn't sure how honed his clean-up skills were.

Once Carlita was gone, Richard crossed his arms and drummed his fingers on his jawbone. "What do we really know about her?"

"Carlita?" I gave him a narrowed-eyed gaze. "The maid your friend Gail has used for years?"

"She was the first person to see the body," Richard said. "What's to say she didn't actually kill Marla and decide to play the hysterical woman card."

"That's rich," Kate said loud enough for Richard to hear her. Since Richard could be more dramatic than almost any woman I'd ever met, her point was a solid one.

As usual, Richard pretended not to hear Kate's comment as he walked into the kitchen and took a wooden cutting board from a hook on the wall. He then took a knife from the block and started cutting wedges of lime. Richard used cooking to calm himself and help him think, so I suspected chopping limes was a way to focus his mind.

"What's her motive?" I asked. "Even if Marla was a terrible boss, which wouldn't surprise me, I doubt that's enough to push someone like Carlita to stab her in the back. Besides, she's a local to the island who works for more than one wealthy, American homeowner. I'm sure she's seen worse than Marla."

"And it was definitely a crime of passion," Leatrice said from where she stood looking out the sliding glass door.

She'd been so quiet since we'd returned from the crime scene, I'd almost forgotten she was there.

"Why are you so sure of that?" Buster asked her.

"The murder weapon was a kitchen knife, and the kitchen was part of the huge, open room in Marla's house." Leatrice turned slowly to face us. "It makes sense that the killer grabbed the knife from the nearby kitchen in a fit of rage and stabbed her in the back."

"You're sure it was a kitchen knife?" Kate asked

I tried to think back to the murder scene. I'd been so distracted by the sight and smell of the blood, I hadn't focused on the details about the knife protruding from the victim's back.

"Positive." Leatrice leveled her arm at Richard as he stood at the counter with a lime in one hand and a black-handled knife in the other. "It was exactly like that one."

Richard slid his gaze to the knife, shrieked, and dropped it to the floor.

CHAPTER 16

"You don't think the knife came from here, do you?" Richard heaved in shallow breaths as he stared at the knife he'd dropped.

"Why would it come from here?" Kate looked unperturbed as she sipped her morning cocktail. "None of us killed her."

"Right." Richard exhaled and bent to retrieve the knife. "I guess it's habit to assume that we'll have evidence planted on us or be framed for a murder we didn't commit."

"That's only happened a few times," I said, although not loudly. I was well aware that being framed for murder one time was not normal, much less, multiple times. "Besides, if Leatrice is right and this was a crime of passion, why would the killer come here to get a knife before stabbing Marla?"

"Do we even have any knives missing?" Kate took a bite of the Mexican breakfast Fern had made, a drop of the salsa lingering on the corner of her lip as she chewed.

"Excellent question." Leatrice strode into the kitchen to examine the knife block and the knives in use, muttering to herself as she counted. "It looks like all our knives are here."

Richard braced his hands on the edge of the counter and heaved out a sigh. "Thank heavens. I would not do well in a Mexican prison."

"Never have truer words been spoken." Fern picked up Kate's Tequila Sunrise, lifted it to Richard in salute, and took a sip.

Richard scowled at this but returned to slicing limes on the wooden cutting board. Fern scooped more beans onto a plate, topped it with a pair of fried eggs, and handed it to me with a wink.

As I inhaled the spicy scent, my stomach growled. Although I couldn't take the smell of fish or smoke, apparently the baby had no issue with salsa. The fried tortilla topped with beans, salsa, and eggs wasn't pretty to look at, but it smelled amazing.

I took a bite, bracing myself for a punch of heat, but the kick never came. I swallowed and moaned with pleasure. "This is really good."

Fern preened from the compliment. "I'm not just a pretty face and perfect hair."

"Same," Kate said through a mouthful of huevos rancheros.

Leatrice tapped one spindly finger on her chin. "It's not surprising that our knife is the same kind as the one used to kill Marla. How many places to buy knives can there be on this island?"

She made a good point. The tiny island had a handful of stores that weren't geared toward tourists and possibly only one or two that would sell housewares. It wasn't a bad assumption that many of the houses shared similar knife blocks. That fact made me wonder. "What if the murder wasn't a crime of passion? What if the killer brought their own knife knowing they were going to kill Marla with it?"

Leatrice's dark, stenciled eyebrows lifted as she nodded. "You make a good point. I don't know that the knife in her back came from her kitchen since we didn't count the knives there."

Richard held up a hand. "Don't even think about it."

"What?" Leatrice's eyes widened to doe-like proportions.

Richard gave her a knowing look. "You know precisely what, and I'm here to say don't even think about going over there again to count knives."

Leatrice's flicker of a frown gave her away. "Fine, but what if the local police don't think to count the knives?"

"Not our problem," Mack said as he joined us again in the kitchen. "We aren't involved in this case, for once."

"That's right." Kate took a long sip of her drink. "This is still my bachelorette celebration, murder or no murder. Not that a dead body isn't on-brand for our crew, but this is going to be one of my last hurrahs before I leave the single life behind. I'd rather not spend it creeping into houses and counting knives."

I grinned at Kate, glad that she was talking about her upcoming wedding, even if it was in a roundabout way. Leatrice, however, did not look happy, but she pressed her lips together and nodded.

"You're right, hon. This getaway is about you." She walked from the kitchen and hopped onto a vacant barstool. "There will be more murders in the future."

"Bite your tongue," Richard said as he shot her a scandalized look.

"She's not the one who wants to get involved," I reminded him.

Richard ignored this comment, gathered his lime wedges in both hands, and plopped them into a blue ceramic bowl.

Fern eyed the bowl. "We're set for garnishes for the next few days."

Richard opened his mouth to respond, but he jumped as his pocket vibrated and chirped. "That had better not be the office. I told them to hold all calls."

I admired the fact that Richard had made himself unavailable for work while we were away. As a small business owner, I knew all too well the temptation to be available for clients around the clock, and with our high-maintenance clientele, that meant there was never a break unless you set a hard line.

Since Kate and I comprised the entirety of Wedding Belles, we'd done our best to work ahead for all of our upcoming brides, and we'd given them ample notice of the office's closure, but I was under no illusions that some bride or her overly nervous mother wouldn't deem cocktail napkins an emergency and call while we were away.

"It's not Grumpy Grace, is it?" Kate asked with a shudder.

One of the brides we shared with Richard never seemed to be in a good mood. Kate swore she'd never seen the woman crack a smile.

Richard made a face. "I strictly forbade her calls from going through." His shoulders relaxed as he pulled out his phone. "It's just Sidney Allen." Then he put a hand to his throat. "There must be something wrong with Hermès. If that man gave him a processed dog biscuit I'll wring his—"

"Love muffin!" Leatrice cried as her husband's face appeared on Richard's phone screen, and she hopped from the stool to stand beside Richard.

"Hello, cupcake." Sidney Allen smoothed his comb-over with one hand, his forehead taking up most of the screen.

"Where's Hermès?" Richard interrupted, swinging the phone to within an inch of his own face. "Is he okay?"

"Hermès?"

Richard gawked at the phone. "My dog? I'm assuming he's the reason you're calling?"

Sidney Allen glanced over his shoulder. "He's asleep. The dog park tired him out."

"Dog park?" Richard's voice dropped a few octaves. "He went to the public dog park?"

"He loves the dog park," Leatrice added. "He gets to see all his friends."

"Friends?" Richard said the word like it was poisonous and swayed a bit.

"His best bud is a terrier mix named Vinnie." Leatrice giggled. "The two of them run around like they're joined at the hip. I mean, Vinnie doesn't run all that fast since he only has the one leg, but Hermès doesn't mind."

The phone slipped from Richard's hand, and Leatrice caught it. I slipped off my stool and put an arm around Richard's shoulders and guided him to the stool Leatrice had vacated.

"My purebred Yorkie has a secret life with Vinnie the one-legged mutt," he mumbled as I pushed him onto the stool.

Kate patted him on the leg. "I've been there."

"If you're not calling about Hermès, why did you call Richard?" Leatrice asked her husband.

"I tried to call you, but you didn't answer."

Leatrice patted her pajamas. "Sorry, cupcake. I must have left my phone in the guesthouse. It's been a little crazy this morning with the murder and all."

Sidney Allen's bulbous eyes became even wider. "Did you say murder?"

I snatched the phone from Leatrice's hand before she could respond. "Nope. No murder. That was just Leatrice trying to speak Spanish. Gotta go. Adios! Vios con dios!"

"Very smooth, Annabelle." Kate gave me a thumbs up. "Not suspicious at all."

Leatrice glanced from me to Kate. "Why can't he know?"

"If you tell him, he might tell her husband and my fiancé, and that will ruin everything," Kate said.

Fern shrugged. "I wouldn't mind the hunky Reese brothers joining our little party."

I sighed. "I don't want to be fussed over any more than I already am, and Kate can't exactly have a last hurrah if her husband-to-be is with her."

"Vinnie?" Richard muttered under his breath. "Why would anyone name a dog Vinnie?"

I clapped my hands to get everyone's attention. "All right people. We need to get it together. No one tells anyone back home about the murder. No one sneaks over to the crime scene." I shot Leatrice a stern look. "And no one says anything to the police that could incriminate us in Marla's murder."

"Why would any of you be incriminated in her murder?"

I yelped and whirled around, dropping the phone at the sight of a uniformed officer standing in the living room.

CHAPTER 17

My heart raced at the sight of the officer with his eyes narrowed and his bushy mustache twitching. "We wouldn't. That was just a figure of speech."

The man's equally bushy brows lifted.

"That's right," Fern waved a saucy spatula at him. "It's like saying we're killing it, which, of course, we are."

I bit back the urge to groan out loud. When my friends jumped in to help, it rarely made me come out looking better. My gaze went to the open front door behind the officer. "Wait, did you just walk in? Is that legal?"

He pivoted to the door. "It was open."

I cut my eyes to Mack, who'd been the last one to close the door when he'd walked out with Carlita. Now that I was looking around, where was Buster?

Mack tentatively lifted his hand into the air. "I might have left the door open since Buster was coming right back after popping into our guesthouse."

I couldn't be angry at him. How was he supposed to know the police would walk in just as I was saying weird things that made us look like suspects? "That's okay." I slapped on my best wedding planner face, the one I used when a client was dancing on my last nerve, but I had to pretend that I didn't want to throttle them. "How can we help you, officer?"

"Huevos rancheros?" Fern held out a plate filled with the increasingly messy dish.

The man shook his head. "I came over to see if you saw anything regarding the murder of your neighbor."

"You mean, aside from her soon-to-be ex-husband standing over her dead body covered in blood?" Leatrice asked, her heavily lined face the picture of innocence.

Richard shot her a scathing look. "He was only covered in blood because he tried to save her."

Leatrice wagged a finger at him. "So he claims."

Richard folded his arms over his chest. "Why would Mr. Bottinger have any reason to kill his ex-wife? She couldn't get the house because of their prenup, and he was willing to give her the settlement she was entitled to in their agreement. All he had to do was wait until the paperwork was finalized and the house would be his. No need to commit murder."

"How do we know that's true?" Leatrice pursed her coral lips. "You know better than to trust what a suspect says."

"She has a point," Kate said. "We've been involved in enough murders to know that suspects lie, especially ones who are guilty of murder."

Richard pressed his lips together until they were a thin line. "We also know that things aren't always what they seem. Just because he looked like he killed her doesn't mean he did it." He pinned Fern with a hard gaze. "Or don't you remember being framed for murder?"

Fern dropped the spatula into the pan, and droplets of salsa splattered onto the stove and counter. "He's got a point. This could be an elaborate setup."

I wasn't sure if I was completely convinced, but I had to admit that it did seem a bit too neat to assume that the ex-husband did it.

A sharply cleared throat brought my attention back to the police officer. "Before you found the suspect standing over the victim, did you see him enter the house?"

We all shook our heads.

"He must have arrived just after she was murdered and right before we found him," I said. "If he is innocent."

"Why do you say that?" The officer's dark eyes were shrewd as he stared at me.

"I saw her, the victim, Marla, not even half an hour before Carlita ran in here screaming that she was dead." I motioned to the pool deck. "I was outside, and I saw her walking inside her house in the same dress we found her wearing when she was killed."

"You are sure?"

I thought back to seeing her pacing through the glass walls of her house. "Same blonde hair, same dress, same voice." I nodded, remembering that shrill voice. "I'm sure."

The man scanned the rest of our group. "Did anyone else see this?"

"Only Annabelle," Fern said. "I was busy cooking; Leatrice was making fake Bloody Marys; Kate was asleep; and Richard was critiquing everything."

Richard sniffed at this but didn't add anything.

"Buster and I walked over from the guesthouse," Mack said, cocking his head. "I think I remember hearing a vehicle next door, but I assumed it was Carlita arriving."

"She did run in screeching not long after that," Leatrice said with a slow shake of her head. "Poor thing, she was a mess."

The officer made a grunting noise in the back of his throat. "That is it?"

"That's pretty much it," I said. "We did see her arguing with a man yesterday before we left for the festival downtown."

"Sandy colored hair, early thirties, works out," Kate added.

"And I saw the shadow of a man late last night arguing with her and then peeling away in a car, but I didn't see his face, so I can't tell you if it was the same guy."

"According to the housekeeper, there were many men." Fern gave the officer a knowing look.

He frowned at this but didn't say anything as he turned and headed for the door.

"So none of us are suspects, right?" Fern asked, as he hurried from the kitchen in his apron and chef's hat that was now slightly askew.

The officer stopped in the doorway and glanced over his shoulder at us. "Why would any of you be suspects when we already have the killer in custody?"

He strode from the house and pulled the door behind him with a resounding thud. We all stood without moving or speaking for a few beats until Fern and Richard spoke at the same time.

"Well, that's a relief!"

"He must be out of his mind!"

They spun toward each other, surprise etched into their faces.

"You really think he's innocent?"

"You can't believe he's guilty!"

Leatrice blinked a few times as her head whipped back and forth.

I stepped between the two divas. "I think we can both agree that it's a relief that none of us are suspects."

"But my client—" Richard started to say.

"Wasn't your client for years," I reminded him. "He broke up with you when he dumped his first wife."

Richard cast me a petulant look. "Technically, Marla broke up with me."

"Should we call back the officer and tell him that?" I tapped one foot on the hard, Mexican tile as Richard grumbled something unintelligible. "I'm not saying that I'm 100 percent convinced that Mr. Bottinger is the killer, but I also know that we can't get involved. We're in a foreign country with very different laws and procedures."

"That never stopped us in Ireland or Bali," Kate said.

Fern held up a finger. "I distinctly remember our lives being in danger both of those times."

"I'd love for our lives not to be in danger this time." I touched a hand to my baby bump.

Richard's shoulders sagged. "Of course, we can't put you and little Gerard at risk." He hurried to me and looped an arm through mine. "Do you want to fly home? I can call the airline right now?"

"I think it's safe to stay." I put my hand over his. "Marla's murder was clearly personal, so it's not like we're in danger from a marauding killer."

A shiver went through Richard. "Even so, we should keep the doors locked and our eyes open."

Fern swung his head from side to side, and the chef's hat flopped even further to one side. "Should we set up a watch schedule so no one can sneak in on us?"

Mack crossed his arms over his chest. "Buster and I can guard the front door."

"I don't think that's necessary." I laughed off my friend's concern. "It's not like there's a serial killer targeting bottle blondes from America."

Kate squeaked and touched a hand to her own blonde bob. "Why would you even say that?"

I sighed. "I said there *isn't* anyone targeting blondes."

"I'm glad I didn't decide to go blonde again." Leatrice patted her own unnaturally jet-black hair that was flipped up at the ends.

"We're all grateful for that," Richard whispered so only I could hear him.

"We're perfectly safe," I said, waving a hand at Mack. "No one is getting past the Mighty Morphin Flower Arrangers."

Richard cleared his throat.

"And Richard," I added.

Fern straightened his white, puffy hat. "I feel better already. Who wants another cocktail?"

My phone trilled in my pocket, and I pulled it out, my stomach sinking when I saw my husband's name flash onto the screen. There wasn't a doubt in my mind why he was calling.

It was times like this I wished my mocktail had been a little less mock.

CHAPTER 18

"Hey, babe!" My voice sounded unnaturally cheery, even to my own ears, as I answered my husband's call while I walked outside to the pool deck.

He was quiet for a moment before he let out a long, tortured sigh. "So, Sidney Allen was right."

"What?" Panic fluttered in my chest. I hadn't even launched into my explanation, and he already knew.

"Tell me about the murder, babe."

As soon as he called me babe, I wilted. "We didn't know it was a murder right away. The lady who cleans the house, Carlita, ran in while Fern was making breakfast and said that the lady next door was dead. It took us questioning Carlita to realize the neighbor had been stabbed."

"The woman who lives next door was stabbed?" His voice was steady, but the tension was unmistakable.

"I know; it's really bad luck. I mean, what are the chances that our neighbor would be murdered only a few days after we arrive?"

"If the past is any indication, extremely high."

I frowned at this, even though he couldn't see me. I walked along the edge of the pool until I was standing under the thatched palapa and shielded from the hot sun blazing overhead. "I swear, we didn't have anything to do with this, and we didn't go looking for trouble, either. We've been trying to avoid Marla since we arrived."

"You knew her name?"

I hesitated before I confessed the next part. "Richard remembered her from a long time ago. She actually lived in DC. Small world, right?"

"Minuscule." He didn't sound happy. "So, Richard knew the victim?" My husband groaned, and I could imagine him scraping a hand across his scruffy cheeks. "Please tell me he isn't a suspect in this."

"He's not. None of us are. We all have airtight alibis since we were with each other, and they already have a suspect in custody."

He released a breath. "That's good. The local police work faster than I would have thought."

I shifted from one foot to the other and rubbed a hand behind my neck as sweat trickled down my spine. "It wasn't much of a challenge. He was found standing over the body with blood on his hands—literally."

"Who is he?

I was glad Mike hadn't noticed that I'd avoided telling him who found the suspect standing over the body, although I doubted I could keep that tidbit from him forever. As a detective trained in interrogation, he had a way of finagling information from me.

"The victim's soon-to-be ex-husband."

"Not surprising. It's usually the husband or wife. I'm guessing the divorce wasn't going well?"

"Not exactly. We heard Marla screaming at him a few times over the phone, even from next door."

"But he ended up being on the island too?"

"With his new girlfriend," I said in a conspiratorial whisper with a glance to the house next door, even though Marla was no longer alive to hear me talking about her and her messy split.

"I guess you aren't in any danger then?" His no-nonsense voice was replaced with one much softer.

"I can't imagine how any of us would be in danger," I said honestly. "If anything, our trip just got less stressful. Marla yelled an awful lot."

He gave a low laugh. "And you feel fine? The baby's okay?"

I put a hand over my bump. "Little Gerard is fine."

He was absolutely silent for a beat. "Please tell me you aren't adding Gerard to the name list."

Now I laughed. "I'm not, although Richard is convinced it's in the running."

"He's also convinced that you've been eating organic the entire pregnancy when I know for a fact that you have a stash of Oreos in the linen closet."

I inhaled sharply. "Don't you dare tell him about my Oreos."

"You know your secret is safe with me," he paused, "as long as you agree to put Veronica back on the baby name list."

"Blackmailer." I walked to the edge of the pool and dipped my bare foot into the water, surprised that it was so refreshing considering the heat of the sun. "Then I get Rose back on the list."

"Rose Reese? We might as well beat her up ourselves before sending her to school."

I stifled a laugh. "You're awful."

"Realistic, babe."

Warmth suffused my chest as I laughed with my husband about baby names, and I almost forgot that he was far away, and I'd seen a dead body not long ago. As much as I loved spending time with my friends, I did miss him.

A bark in the background made me straighten. "Is Hermès with you?"

"Well, Sidney Allen brought him when he came to tell me about your weird phone call." He dropped his voice. "And now he won't leave."

I'd had the same problem with Leatrice since I'd moved into the building, and my husband had always found it somewhat amusing when she'd show up at all hours in various outlandish outfits. Her husband seemed to have inherited the habit, although I suspected it was for the same reasons. "I'm sure he's just lonely without his honeybun."

Mike huffed out a breath. "It's going to be crowded in here when Daniel arrives to watch the game."

"I don't know. It sounds like a fun guys' afternoon."

"Sidney Allen is wearing a smoking jacket and an ascot," he whispered, "and we're watching rugby."

"I was going to tell you I miss you, but I'm definitely glad I'm missing that, although Sidney Allen will class up the sport." Then I paused. "Please tell me the dog isn't also wearing an ascot."

"I wish I could, babe. I wish I could." He released a tormented breath, then his voice regained its stern edge. "Promise me that if anything else happens, you'll tell me."

I hesitated. "Anything? I'm with Fern, Kate, and Leatrice. Things are going to happen."

"You know what I mean. Promise me you won't get caught up in any murder drama."

That was pretty broad, but I actually had no desire to get involved with this case. I hadn't liked the victim; none of my friends were suspects; and I really did want to get some relaxation in before the baby arrived. "I promise."

That wasn't even a lie. I intended to stay far from the murder case. Now what Richard did was entirely up to him, and I did not have a great feeling that he could make the same promise.

CHAPTER 19

When I returned inside, my friends had mostly scattered. Fern was still in the kitchen alongside Richard, who was muttering to himself as he cleaned up the disastrous counters, and Kate was sitting on a barstool spinning around in slow circles.

"How's the hunky hubby?" Fern asked as he gave me a sly smile.

"He's good." I held up a hand as Richard spun around. "And before you ask, yes, he's checked on Hermès and the dog is also fine. He's watching rugby."

Kate stopped spinning. "The dog or your husband?"

"Both. Sidney Allen came upstairs to rat me out to Mike and brought Hermès. Now they're all watching rugby." I waved a finger at Kate. "And your husband-to-be is on his way to join them."

Kate's brow lifted in mild interest but instead of replying, she spun to face the other way and reached for her Tequila Sunrise.

"Rugby." Richard shook his head in obvious disapproval. "Such toxic masculinity isn't good for a sensitive creature like Hermès."

"If it helps, he's wearing an ascot while watching, so I'm pretty sure that negates any hypermasculinity." I decided not to mention that if the Yorkie was hanging out with mixed breed dogs from the park named Vinnie, then TV habits weren't Richard's biggest concern.

"Did he know?" Kate asked, twisting around again with drink in hand.

"About the murder?" I joined her at the counter and hopped onto a stool. "Oh, yeah. Apparently, Sidney Allen didn't buy my lame cover story or believe that Leatrice was speaking Spanish. He went right upstairs to tell Mike that she'd said there was a murder."

Fern plucked the chef's hat from his head and smoothed his dark hair, which was still in a flawless topknot. "So, when should we expect him?"

"We shouldn't." I picked up a fork and poked at my now cold huevos rancheros, wishing I'd eaten the dish when it was hot. "I managed to convince him not to worry since we weren't going to get involved with this case."

"You lied?" Kate made a clicking noise with her tongue. "I thought part of your wedding vows included 'I shall not get involved in criminal investigations.'"

"Ha ha. He wishes." I took a bite of the slightly congealed eggs and salsa-soaked tortillas. "But I didn't lie. I'm not getting mixed up in this murder."

Kate, Richard, and Fern all stared at me, the disbelief etched on their faces.

"What?" I took a sip of my virgin Bloody Mary, which was just tomato juice with a stalk of celery. "Aside from finding her ex-husband standing over Marla's dead body, I have zero intention of meddling."

Kate tapped a pink-polished nail on her jaw. "When have I heard that before?"

"The only reason I got involved in cases before was because either I was implicated," I pulled the celery from my drink and pointed it at each of the trio in turn, "or one of you was. That isn't the case this time. Not only did I not care much for the victim, but I also don't have any connection to the suspect. Thankfully, none of us are even close to being implicated in this murder."

"Knock on wood." Fern quickly rapped his knuckles on the cutting board, and Richard followed his lead.

"You forget something, darling." Richard swept a handful of kitchen scraps off the counter and into his open palm. "I know the suspect, and he personally requested that I help him."

"Which I think is a bad idea." I took a bite from the leafy end of the celery. "You haven't worked for this guy for over a decade, and now he comes crying to you for help. If you ask me, that's typical entitled-client crap."

Fern bobbed his head in agreement. "I have to side with Annabelle here. What do you really owe this man? When he left his first wife for Marla, did he try to keep you on as his caterer? Did he stick his neck out for anyone, or did he roll over and do whatever his new wife wanted?" Fern folded his arms over his chest. "He's shown you who he is, sweetie. Just because he's desperate doesn't mean he should be able to snap his fingers and make you come running."

Richard drew himself up to his full height. "Are you implying that I'm a dog?"

Considering how much he adored and pampered his pooch, I wasn't sure why he was taking such offense, but I held my palms up. "I think Fern is just worried that Mr. Bottinger is taking advantage."

"I prefer to think that he's realized the error of his ways now that he's not under Marla's influence," Richard said. "Besides, someone has to cater his parties in the future."

"If they hold soirees in cell block one," Fern whispered.

Richard swung his head and pinned Fern with a look that could kill. "We all agree that Mr. Bottinger didn't have the motive to kill her, which means the actual killer is out there. I don't know about you, but I couldn't live with myself if I let an innocent man with a huge entertaining budget rot in jail and let a murderer go free."

"I can live with myself if I'm not the one finding the real killer. Besides, I promised my husband I wouldn't get involved." I leveled a hard gaze at Richard. "And you promised to make sure I didn't do anything dangerous."

Richard emitted a tortured groan. "Fine. You can't get involved. I guess that means I need to find someone else to help me."

He glanced at Kate and Fern, who both shook their heads.

Kate held up her drink. "I'm the bachelorette."

"And I'm in charge of making sure the bride-to-be has fun." Fern wrinkled his nose. "Murder isn't fun."

"You know who would love to be your assistant?" I grinned at Richard. "Or should I say, crime-fighting sidekick?"

Richard closed his eyes for a beat. "Heaven preserve me."

"You couldn't find anyone more enthusiastic," I reminded him as I reveled in his internal turmoil.

Kate's face brightened as she realized who I meant. "You really couldn't. Plus, she's got all the disguises you could need if you have to go undercover."

Richard opened his eyes and glared at all of us. "You must have lost your minds if you think I'm going to involve Leatrice in my attempts to clear Mr. Bottinger."

"Your loss. When I was a fugitive from the law and almost had to go on the lam, Leatrice was a great sidekick." Fern gave him a saccharine smile as he flounced from the kitchen. "Now, as the cruise director of fun, I promised our bachelorette lunch in town, so I need to change."

"Lunch in town sounds good." I gave up eating my cold breakfast and dropped my fork onto the plate.

"I suppose that would give me the opportunity to check on my client at the jail." Richard held up a finger as I opened my mouth. "By myself."

I didn't say anything as he stomped off, but given my past experience, I doubted that he would be able to do anything regarding the case without having Leatrice close on his heels. I was just glad I wouldn't have to be involved.

"Does it feel strange to not be in the middle of the case?" Kate asked when we were the only two left in the kitchen.

I took a final swig of tomato juice as my stomach fluttered. "Actually, I have zero desire to get involved."

"Not even if it means we'd get a crack at the third Bottinger wedding?"

I shuddered. "Not on your life. I'm only interested in one wedding at the moment."

Kate's bright smile faded as she interpreted my pointed look. "Not this again."

I gaped at her. "This again? You mean, your wedding? The entire reason we're here?" I grabbed her stool and spun her to face me. "Okay, spill it. What's going on? Why are you being so weird about your wedding?"

She raked a hand through her hair and met my gaze. "Don't you remember how strange it was to be a bride when you got married? After getting so many brides down the aisle, it doesn't feel right to be the one on the other side."

I eyed her. I did remember the odd sensation, but her reaction didn't feel like that. "Is that it?"

Her shoulder sagged. "I never thought I'd be the kind of girl to get married. I'd all but decided that I'd be a career single girl. The kind of girl who's a great aunt to all her friends' kids but who never settles down. I imagined myself being a free agent forever, and now I won't be."

"And that's a bad thing?" I asked softly.

She met my eyes with blue ones filled with tears. "What if I'm not good at it? What if I've been single for so long that I'm a terrible wife, and I break his heart and ruin his life?"

"You would never do that on purpose." I grabbed her hands and squeezed them. "And Daniel will never do that to you. He isn't your ex. He will never cheat on you or break your heart. One thing I know about Reese men is that they're loyal to a fault. They're also stubborn and overprotective, but that's a whole other story."

She nodded, her lips twitching as tears spilled down her cheeks. "My brain knows that but my heart…"

"It's okay to be scared. Getting married and making big promises is scary, but it's also completely worth it." I smiled at her. "Besides, I've seen the way Daniel looks at you. You could be a horrible cook, a terrible housekeeper, and snore like a freight train, and he wouldn't care."

She sniffled. "Good, because most of that is true."

"I know." I pulled her into a hug. "Honestly, I'm relieved he agreed to take you off our hands, because as cute as you are, you are not an easy sell."

Kate pulled back from me and burst into laughter. "Thanks, boss."

"I think you mean partner." I gave her shoulders a quick squeeze. "Now let's go get ready for lunch. I'm starving."

"What are you two doing still sitting there?" Fern bustled from one side of the house in a brightly striped sarape with white fringe. "I'll pull the golf cart around while you change."

Kate and I exchanged a look as he strode toward the door with the bell sleeves of the colorful garment flapping. It was going to be an interesting lunch.

CHAPTER 20

"I don't know how you did it," I told Richard as we watched Leatrice and Fern disappear down a pedestrian street in the island's small downtown. I'd been so sure Leatrice would insist on accompanying Richard everywhere since she knew he was determined to help Mr. Bottinger clear his name.

"It wasn't Richard." Kate led the way to a restaurant with outside seating and an awning that shaded the tables from the sun. "Leatrice wanted one of those sarapes."

I bit back a groan of dismay at the thought of both Fern and Leatrice walking around like they should be riding on the back of donkeys and wearing sombreros. Neither of them had ever gotten the memo about cultural appropriation.

"We need to save them seats," I reminded my friends as we were led to a table for six and handed menus.

"I'm still surprised that Buster and Mack opted to skip lunch." Kate slid her sunglasses to the top of her head.

"I'm not." Richard leaned back and crossed his legs, his perfectly pressed ecru pants making me even more self-conscious about my wrinkled sundress. "They were expecting a call from Prue, and you know how obsessed they are about her and Merry."

I thought it was bold for him to call anyone else obsessed when his dog wore a Burberry collar, but I didn't say anything. I was too distracted by the intoxicating aroma of food that wafted from the restaurant to focus on much else, and my stomach rumbled again.

Richard glanced over and frowned. "You aren't eating enough. Clearly, I'm going to have to take over cooking duties at the house."

"You didn't like Fern's breakfast?" Kate asked.

"You mean what didn't end up on the floor?" Richard made a face. "By the time he was done, he'd gone through all our eggs and every pan in the kitchen."

"I thought it was pretty good when it was warm." I quickly scanned the menu and decided on tacos al pastor since I was sure the pork, onion, and pineapple combination wouldn't trigger nausea.

The waitress came over with glasses of water for us, which I eagerly sipped as Kate ordered a mango margarita and Richard ordered guacamole for the table. Even though we were shaded, the sun was still hot and high in the colorless sky, and I concentrated on not moving much so I wouldn't sweat.

"I hope it doesn't take long to buy a sarape," I said as I glanced down the street lined with souvenir shops, jewelry boutiques, and restaurants.

"I hope that's all they buy," Richard muttered. "I am not flying home with anyone wearing a Mexican hat." Then he sucked in a quick breath as his eyes popped open.

"What?" I craned my neck as I glanced around for Leatrice and Fern in enormous felt hats with gold trim.

Richard reached over and put his hand over mine. "Look who it is."

I swiveled my head around again, but I was clearly missing something. At this point, Kate was also swinging her head from side to side. "Who? Where?"

Richard narrowed his eyes at us. "You two need to work on your subtly." He jerked his head to one side. "It's Mr. B's girlfriend."

I followed his line of sight to the young blonde sitting at a nearby table in the same restaurant. It took me a beat to realize that Mr. B was Mr. Bottinger.

I leaned over to him and kept my voice low. "Are you sure?"

He nodded. "I recognize the huge diamond on her finger."

I snuck another glance at the woman, noticing the enormous margarita glass in front of her that was nearly empty. Her hands were wrapped around the glass, and one finger glittered with an impressive solitaire diamond. "So, the girlfriend is actually a fiancée?"

"And the fiancée looks pretty drunk," Kate added.

"It's barely noon." Now that she mentioned it, the woman's eyes did look glassy, and she was slumped forward like someone who had enjoyed one too many cocktails.

"She must be drowning her sorrows." Kate eyed the blonde who hadn't seemed to notice us studying her. "And she's alone, which means that her sugar daddy must still be in jail."

Richard flinched at the term 'sugar daddy' but he didn't argue. "Poor girl. We should invite her to join us. We have an extra chair."

I slid a suspicious gaze to my friend. "Your altruism knows no bounds."

He ignored my deadpanned statement while waving a hand in the air to catch the woman's attention. "Join us!"

She appeared slightly startled, but either she was too polite to ignore us, or she was tired of being alone, because she picked up her nearly empty drink and weaved her way over to our table.

"Sit." Richard hopped up and pulled out the chair next to him on the other side. "I'm Richard, and this is Annabelle and Kate."

"Victoria," the woman said with a crooked smile. "Thanks for inviting me to sit with you."

"Don't mention it." Richard waved her thanks away with one hand. "No need for a fellow American to dine alone. Where are you from, sweetie?"

"Originally, Kansas." She stared into the remnants of her margarita. "But now I live in DC."

"So do we!" Richard's manufactured surprise was almost too much, but luckily Victoria was too drunk to notice.

"You do?" She looked up at us. "Small world."

"We're here celebrating this one's bachelorette." Richard jerked a thumb at Kate without taking his gaze off Victoria.

"Congratulations," Victoria managed to say with minimal slurring. She held up her left hand and wiggled her fingers. "Me too. Engaged, that is. I'm not celebrating my bachelorette." She sighed and took a swig of her drink, draining almost the last of it. "I was supposed to be celebrating getting engaged, but that didn't really work out."

Richard assumed an expression of mock confusion. "Why not?"

She hiccupped and put a hand over her mouth. "My fiancé got arrested."

"No!" Richard recoiled with such force that he almost tipped his chair over.

Kate shot him a look as she gave the woman a look of genuine sympathy. "That's awful."

The waitress arrived with our drinks and guacamole, placing the rough stone mortar in the center of the table along with two baskets of chips that were so fresh that oil glistened off them.

"Why don't I order you another drink?" Richard asked, while motioning to the waitress for another margarita for our new friend.

Victoria bobbed her head in agreement as she plucked a chip from the basket. "He's innocent, of course. Victor would never hurt a soul."

"Victor?" I almost choked on the hot, salty chip I'd just bitten into. "Your fiancé's name is Victor?"

She giggled. "I know. Isn't it perfect? Victor and Victoria. He said it meant we were made for each other."

I fought the urge to roll my eyes and gag simultaneously.

"Am I having a musical theatre fever dream?" Richard murmured into his drink as I tried to talk over him.

"How did you two meet?"

She shifted in her chair. "I was his wife's yoga instructor."

Richard's mouth fell open while Kate almost spluttered her mango margarita.

"It's not how it sounds, though," Victoria said quickly. "His marriage was already over when he met me, and believe me, I didn't blame him for wanting to leave her. She was the meanest client I've ever had."

"So, he got a divorce and then you started dating?" Richard asked, nudging the fresh margarita toward her once the waitress set it down.

"Something like that," she said once she'd lifted the wide-rimmed glass to her lips. "Although you'd have thought I stole him from her the way Marla went after me."

I had no problem imagining Marla's reaction when she'd found out that her husband had been cheating on her with her nubile yoga instructor who was basically a younger, bendier version of her. I took another addictively salty chip and dipped it in the guacamole while Kate and Richard exchanged glances over the woman's head.

"What do you mean, went after you?" Kate asked.

Victoria's face darkened. "That witch tried to ruin me. She told all of her rich socialite friends that I was a husband stealer, so my private clientele dried up. No one wants to hire a private yoga instructor who sleeps with her clients' husbands."

"I wouldn't think so," I said through a mouthful of deliciously creamy guacamole.

"What?" Victoria glanced at me and cocked her head.

"She said she wishes she could drink more," Richard said before I could respond, turning back to Victoria. "But you were saying how your fiancé's wife ruined your life."

"Right." Victoria took another gulp of her cocktail. "She would have ruined everything if she could have, but Victor took care of it."

Richard froze. "Took care of it?"

"That's why we're here." The blonde rested her chin on the palm of one hand as she leaned her elbows on the wooden table. "Victor agreed to pay her off if she would stop posting things online about me and bombing my Yelp profile with one-star reviews."

Kate cut a wide-eyed look to me and we both looked at Richard, whose face had drained of color.

"They were negotiating a payoff?" Richard's voice was tight.

"A big one." Victoria lowered her voice. "I felt bad that Victor was giving her so much to shut her up, but he said I was worth it. Isn't he the best?" Then she shrugged one shoulder. "Not that he has to worry about paying her now."

The chip Richard was holding in his hand shattered into pieces.

CHAPTER 21

"Breathe," I told Richard as he stood inside a souvenir shop with his hands braced on his knees.

He peered up at me between a standing display of straw hats with "Viva Mexico!" stitched on them and a rack of colorfully embroidered backpacks. "Didn't you hear her? She practically implicated Mr. Bottinger in his wife's murder."

He had a point, but the blonde had also been pretty tipsy, so I wasn't sure if we could rely on her completely.

Richard straightened and held up his fingers. "First, she admitted that they started an affair before he was divorced, and it sounds like before they were even separated. Then she said that Marla tried to ruin her, which gives Mr. B even more motive." He ticked off two fingers. "But the sombrero on top was her saying that he came here to pay off Marla and now doesn't have to because she's dead!"

A passerby gave us both a startled look, but I smiled and waved before swinging back to Richard. "I hate to give you any reason to get more involved, but none of those mean he killed her.

Sure, we now know of more motives, but it's just as possible that Victoria killed Marla."

Richard tilted his head to one side. "You're right. Blondie is the one who actually stands to gain the most from Marla's death, doesn't she?"

I wasn't sure if I'd have put it that way. It seemed like the husband would be saving a ton of money and headaches with his ex gone, but there was no doubt the new fiancée had plenty of motives herself. "My point is that we don't know the entire story. Neither do the Mexican authorities."

Richard's eyes widened. "Should we tell them what we know?"

"It depends if you want to put the final nail in Mr. B's proverbial coffin or not."

"Right." He shook his head, even though his perfectly spiked, dark hair didn't budge. "Victoria's information does not make him look good."

"Why don't we go back and have lunch before our new friend starts to get suspicious." I nodded toward the restaurant next door.

"I'm not sure if she's bright enough or sober enough to be suspicious, but you're right." He smoothed his hands down the front of his pale blue button-down that wasn't even remotely damp. "It doesn't do my client any good for me to be hiding out next to T-shirts that say 'Number Juan Dad'. I need to go to the source."

I blinked at him. The source for what?

He patted the side of my arm. "You go back and eat. I'm going to talk to Mr. Bottinger."

My first instinct was to tell him I'd go with him. That was what I would have done in the past, but I'd promised Mike that I wouldn't let myself get pulled into a murder investigation. And, I reminded myself, I didn't want to get involved. I wanted to eat chips and guacamole, drink fake fruity drinks, and float in the pool. Even if every problem-solving urge in my brain was firing, I knew I couldn't do it.

"Fine," I said as we stepped from the shop and onto the pedestrian street. "You go to the jail. I'll see what else I can find out from Victoria."

"Jail?" Leatrice's shrill voice made me jump. "Why is Richard going to jail?"

As I'd feared, my octogenarian neighbor was wearing a brightly striped sarape that was an almost identical match to the one Fern wore as he stood next to her. Sadly, she was so much smaller than him, her fringed poncho looked like a dress as it swung around her calves.

"He's going to visit his former client who's still the prime suspect in Marla's murder," I said, a smile stretching across my face. "I can't go with him, but you can."

Leatrice bounced on the balls of her feet as Richard pinned me with a death glare. "I don't think I've ever been inside a jail. Certainly not one in a foreign country. This is going to be so exciting."

"You won't be in the jail cell," I said before sliding my gaze to Richard. "Right?"

His look was murderous as Leatrice twittered on about visiting the slammer. "I make no promises, darling."

I looped my arm through Fern's. "You and I have a drunk bachelorette to question." I glanced over at the table where Kate sat with her arm thrown over Victoria's shoulders as the two women clinked oversized margarita glasses. "Make that two drunk bachelorettes."

Fern winked at me. "My specialty."

Before I could issue more warnings to Leatrice, Richard was off, and she was hurrying along beside him. I turned back to the restaurant, knowing that, despite Richard's constant grumbling about my nosy neighbor, he was fond of her in his own way. That didn't mean I was totally convinced he wouldn't leave her in a jail cell if he got the chance, but on the flip side, she would probably think it was a hoot. Then I remembered what she was wearing and started worrying again.

Fern led the way to the table, ordering himself a margarita on the rocks as he passed the waitress, who blinked at the sarape he wore belted at the waist.

"What are we drinking to?" he asked as he took the chair across from the two women.

"Fern!" Kate cried out then leaned into Victoria's ear. "This is the best wedding hairstylist in DC. Whatever you do for your wedding, you must hire him."

Victoria's green eyes bugged out. "You're *the* Fern?"

Fern preened as he pretended to brush away the comment. "Yes, but I don't like people to make a fuss."

There was little Fern loved more than people making a fuss.

"You're legendary," Victoria said in a reverent tone. "I hear you book up a year in advance."

"True." Fern touched a hand to his hair and flashed the enormous blue topaz ring that looked like a glittering egg perched on his finger. "But I can always squeeze in a friend."

"Victoria is definitely a friend," Kate said, then gave an exaggerated frown. "But we don't know when or if her wedding is happening."

"No!" Fern pressed a hand to his throat and appeared genuinely shocked.

Then I remembered that he had no idea who the blonde with Kate was or why we'd befriended her. It was probably for the best since he wasn't always great at keeping secrets or being secretive.

Kate dropped her voice to a conspiratorial whisper. "Her fiancé isn't divorced yet, and he's in jail."

Fern took the fresh margarita from the waitress before she could put it down. "I think you might need a new fiancé, sweetie."

Victoria shook her head. "No, Victor is wonderful, but I just realized he doesn't need a divorce anymore."

Fern's eyes bulged from his head. "Are you going to be in one of those sister-wife families?"

"No." She looked genuinely perplexed. "He doesn't need a divorce because his ex-wife died this morning."

Fern paused mid-sip, his expression stunned. "How many people have died on this island today?"

"Only one," I said from the side of my mouth and behind my cupped hand. "This is Marla's husband's new fiancée."

Fern took a significant gulp. "I think I'm going to need another one of these."

"Can I tell you a secret?" Victoria leaned over the table and darted a nervous gaze around the sparsely populated restaurant.

Fern also leaned forward. "There's nothing we love more than a secret."

"I'm convinced that his wife is haunting me." Victoria emitted an agitated laugh. "Which is exactly the kind of vindictive thing Marla would do." She slammed her hand on the table. "Her ghost is haunting me from the grave."

We all stared at her until Fern broke the silence by taking a loud slurp of his drink. "I'm not an expert on this, but I don't think she can haunt you from the grave if she isn't in one yet."

Victoria hiccupped and flapped her hand in the air. "Then why is she still following me?"

CHAPTER 22

"She didn't mean that she actually thinks Marla's ghost is following her, did she?" Buster asked once we'd returned to the house and joined him and Mack at the pool. The two men were slathered in suntan oil, which made their bald heads look even glossier as they bobbed in the pool overlooking the ocean. The sun was finally sinking lower into the sky, but it was still blazing hot, and the air carried the scent of salt water and Banana Boat, with a hint of chlorine.

I shook my head as I sat on the edge of the pool with the bottom half of my legs dangling in the water and my sundress hitched up around my thighs. "Apparently, Marla accosted her and Mr. B last night at the festival. She was wearing her wedding dress and a full face of that skeleton makeup. I think in Victoria's permanent state of inebriation since her fiancé was arrested, she's convinced that everyone dressed like a Dias de los Meurtos bride is Marla's ghost coming back to haunt her."

Mack shivered from where he lay on a green, inflatable float that was barely above water and rubbed his bare, tattooed arms. "Well, that's a terrifying thought."

Kate lifted the edge of her oversized straw hat to peer at us with one eye open as she stretched out on a lounge chair. "I feel bad for the girl. Marla terrorized her and destroyed her business. I'm not surprised she thinks the old crone is still after her."

I didn't remind Kate that technically Victoria had started an affair with Marla's husband before they were separated, so she wasn't the only wronged party. But I'd also met both the almost-ex-wife and the new fiancée, and didn't blame Mr. B for picking the pretty, sweet blonde over the shrill, vindictive one.

Fern fanned himself with the latest copy of *Vanity Fair* as he lay in the lounger next to Kate's. "Imagine getting engaged and then having your fiancé end up in jail for murdering his ex-wife for you. It's so romantic."

"Romantic?" I made a face and swiped at the sweat on my upper lip. "Since when is murdering someone considered a romantic gesture?"

"I know the anniversary for the first year of marriage is paper." Kate reached for her margarita glass, which she'd filled with a slapdash cocktail of vodka and all the juices she could find. "Which year is murder?"

"This is the groom's third wedding, so maybe the rules are different." Fern giggled as he picked up his cocktail. "Maybe the gift for engagements for third weddings is murder?"

"He didn't commit murder," Richard said as he strode outside with Leatrice close on his heels.

We all turned toward him as he dropped his towel on a chair and walked into the pool in his black designer swim trunks that I was certain were more expensive than everything I'd packed.

"You're back." My gaze went quickly from him to Leatrice who was dressed in a pink hibiscus print two-piece bathing suit and a swim cap covered in matching pink flowers. Between the bright flowers and the significant amount of wrinkled skin, I wasn't sure where to look first.

"Taxis aren't thick on the ground here." Richard shot me a look as he submerged himself up to his chin.

"I texted you when we were done with lunch." I scissored my feet in the water. "You said you needed more time."

"We did." Leatrice stepped into an inflatable child's pool ring sitting on the pool deck and easily pulled it to her waist. "Mr. Bottinger was a fount of information."

"And that fount convinced you he's innocent?" I asked as Richard began to swim the breaststroke across the length of the rectangular pool. Buster and Mack both paddled their rafts and floats out of his path.

Richard didn't turn his head. "I already knew he was innocent."

Leatrice stepped gingerly down the steps of the pool until she was bobbing in the float with her spindly arms draped over the pink plastic.

"What about what I texted you that his fiancée said?" I asked.

Richard reached the wall. If someone could turn in a huff in a pool, he did. "You mean that drunk bimbo?"

Kate sat up. "She's not a bimbo, and she wasn't that drunk."

"As much as I loved seeing Merry and Prue on FaceTime, I'm starting to be sad we missed lunch," Mack said to Buster as he paddled by him in his float.

Richard cocked an eyebrow that clearly said he disagreed with Kate's assessment. "I hardly think the word of a yoga instructor who had just as much motive to kill Marla is going to carry much weight. Besides, who's to say she didn't say all those things to implicate him so she doesn't look like the prime suspect she is?"

He made a point. Victoria did have reason to want Marla gone from their lives, although if her fiancé was going to pay off his ex, then it didn't make sense that Victoria would feel the need to commit murder. Her fiancé was solving her problems. He was the only one who benefitted the most from a dead soon-to-be ex. "How did he explain that he was going to Marla's to pay her off and then she ended up dead?"

"He says that never happened," Leatrice said before Richard could reply.

Fern stopped fanning himself. "Victoria lied to us?"

"Mr. Bottinger says that his fiancée must have misunderstood. Marla did make lots of threats, but that was par for the course. He says he told Victoria he would take care of it, but he only meant that he would remind Marla of their prenup, which was what he'd gone to her place to do."

It sounded to me like Mr. B was full of empty promises. Considering the fact that he had two wives and a third one in the wings, and that he'd cheated on all of his exes, I had a hard time believing what he'd told Richard. Chances were good he told the women in his life what he thought they wanted to hear whether it was the truth or not.

"Your client still sounds like he has the most to gain from Marla's death," I told Richard.

"And why was he here with his new fiancée?" Leatrice asked, the rubber flower petals on her swim cap jiggling. "Did he do it to torture Marla or to have someone he could cast blame on once he'd murdered her?"

Richard stopped his precise breaststroke and gave her a look of one who'd been betrayed. "I thought you believed Mr. Bottinger?"

Leatrice fluttered her bony legs behind her in the water. "I did when he was talking. He's very charming and convincing, but now that Annabelle brings up these points, I'm having doubts."

"I remember Mr. B from an event we did at his office." Buster swiped a hand across the top of his oiled head. "He was charming. So charming he was slick."

"That's most of the wealthy men in DC." Richard cut his gaze to me for a beat. "And let's all remember that, per her request, Annabelle is not part of this investigation."

I sighed. I guess he was still holding a grudge for me sticking him with Leatrice. "I might not be running around to jails and crashing murder scenes, but I did just spend an hour talking to a potential witness."

"A drunk witness," Richard muttered as he resumed his laps.

He had a point. As much as I thought Victoria was sincere, she had been pretty hammered at lunch. If we wanted to know what she knew, we'd have to question her when she was sober. Correction, I thought. The police would have to question her. I was not investigating.

"Well, that drunk witness just texted me." Kate held up her phone screen.

"How does she have your number?" I asked.

"Fern and I both gave her our numbers." Kate tapped at the screen. "I thought she might need another bride-to-be to talk to."

"And I thought her hair needed help." Fern made a face. "Did you see her roots?"

"So she's not a natural blonde?" Leatrice asked.

"As natural as you were, sweetie." Fern winked at her, and I cringed as I remembered my neighbor's brief foray into life as a platinum blonde.

"Don't tell me she's had another sighting of the ghost of Marla," I said.

"The what?" Leatrice jerked up so fast she almost slipped through the inflatable ring.

"Victoria thinks she's being haunted by Marla's ghost," Kate said without looking up. "The rest of us think she's being unduly influenced by all the Dias de los Muertos brides."

"This is why the woman is an unreliable witness," Richard said.

"Unreliable or not, she isn't texting about a ghost sighting."

Leatrice's shoulders sagged. Ghost sightings were exactly her idea of a good time.

"Does she need drinking buddies for happy hour?" Fern asked, already swinging his legs off the lounge chair.

Kate shook her head. "She says she has something she needs to tell us. Something she didn't tell us at lunch."

"I hope it's her skin care secrets, because she doesn't have a wrinkle on her face." Fern patted his own cheeks.

"Not many teenagers do," I said, even though I knew the woman was in her twenties.

Fern smiled at me. "Touché, sweetie."

"She says she has something to tell us about Marla." Kate looked up from her phone and slid her sunglasses down her nose to reveal wide eyes. "Something about her murder."

CHAPTER 23

"How do we know she's telling the truth?" I asked as we all sat inside the house after showering and changing. The sun was sinking lower toward the horizon, and golden light was streaming through the windows.

"Why would she lie?" Kate asked, tucking her bare legs under her and running her hand through her freshly washed, damp hair.

Richard sipped on his glass of ice water. "I thought we already established that she's setting up my client."

"Former client," I said in a stage whisper.

Richard ignored this. "I think the best idea is not to respond to the message. If Mr. Bottinger's fiancée has anything important regarding the case, she should go to the police, especially if it vindicates her fiancé."

Fern leaned forward from his perch on the end of the couch. "What if she can't go to the police?"

"Why wouldn't she be able to go to the police?" Richard asked. "She managed to get herself to the restaurant, and that's right around the corner from the jail."

"I don't know." Fern sat back. "I feel like that's something people say when they have crucial information. They can't go to the police because either they won't be believed, or the cops are in on it."

"I don't think the cops are in on it." Buster sat in a low armchair, his bulk overflowing the sides. "There aren't enough of them on the island to make a decent conspiracy."

Leatrice sat on one end of the couch in a Mexican peasant dress, nodding thoughtfully. "Maybe she doesn't think she'll be believed."

Richard released a frustrated sigh. "Why wouldn't she be believed?"

"If she knows something that makes her fiancé seem even guiltier, she might not want to tell the cops, especially since Mr. B probably has an expensive lawyer who will get him out, and she has nothing." I thought about the story she'd told us. "She has no business anymore, so she's completely dependent on her husband-to-be."

"Which is exactly why she wouldn't want to incriminate him," Kate said. "If he goes away for murder, she's out a husband and a sugar daddy."

"So we're back to square one." Mack stood up, his leather pants creaking as he headed for the kitchen. "We have no idea why the woman would text Kate and say she has some information about the murder."

"You mean aside from the fact that she knows no one else on the island who isn't in jail, and Kate was nice to her?" I rested my hands on my belly, grateful to be out of the heat. "As far as I could see, she doesn't speak Spanish, so we can't discount the fact that she might be intimidated by the Mexican authorities."

Richard made a sound in the back of his throat that I knew meant he thought I might be right but wouldn't say it out loud.

"So, you think I should meet her?" Kate asked, looking at her phone like it might bite her.

"Definitely," Leatrice said.

At the same time, Richard said, "Absolutely not."

"You won't have to go alone," Leatrice bounced in place. "I'll go with you."

"It goes without saying that I'll go," Fern added, patting her on the arm. "Especially if we go to happy hour right after."

The thought of going downtown again and then to another restaurant made me want to curl up into a ball and go to sleep, but that was an urge I had constantly. Aside from the baby wanting me to eat more, it also required naps. Many naps.

"Why does she require a meeting?" Richard asked. "Why can't she text you the information?"

Kate shrugged. "She said she needs to tell me in person."

"Maybe she doesn't want to go on record for revealing it," Fern said in a hush.

That made sense, but I couldn't imagine who she would want to hide her revelation from, if not her fiancé. Richard must have thought the same thing because he huffed out an impatient breath.

"This is all a bunch of smoke and mirrors. I'll bet her secret is nothing but some rumor."

"What if it isn't?" Leatrice scooted to the edge of the couch. "What if it's the key to solving the entire thing?"

Richard stood suddenly. "Fine. I know I'll never hear the end of it if we don't find out what this silly woman has to say."

I stared at him. "Does that mean you're going too?"

He slid his gaze to Leatrice and Fern then back to me. "Well, I'm not going to leave it up to them."

Leatrice bounded to her feet, clearly not even the slightest bit insulted by Richard's assessment of her. "The more, the merrier."

"Buster groaned as he stood. "I'm not missing the chance for dinner out."

"So, you're all going to the secret meeting with a witness who might hold a vital clue to the murder investigation?" When I only got nods and smiles all around, I pushed myself to my feet. "Then I'm not staying here by myself."

As we walked from the house and piled into golf carts, I wondered if Victoria had any idea what she'd gotten herself into when she'd texted Kate. The poor woman probably had no clue that our motley crew was going to descend on her like a weirdly dressed swarm.

As Mack stepped on the gas and our cart lurched forward, I turned around to Kate, who was in the back with Fern. "Are we meeting her at the same restaurant?"

We drove up the pebbled driveway and onto the narrow, paved road that ran in front of the house, with Kate gripping the bar overhead to keep from falling out. "No. She said that was too busy."

I didn't recall the place being overly populated when we'd been there, but I hadn't been to the venue during evening hours, and I'd heard that many of the restaurants got bustling at happy hour. "So where are we meeting her? A hotel? An AirBnB?"

"I don't think it's a hotel," Kate said loud enough to be heard over the rumble of the golf cart's motor as we drove along the road that hugged the coast and passed more impressive houses fronting the water. "She sent me the address, so I popped it into Google Maps."

If Mr. Bottinger wasn't staying at one of the few luxury resorts on Isla Mujeres, then he must have booked a fancy AirBnB or maybe a luxury condo on the beach. I knew the house he owned had been occupied by Marla, but there must be other equally impressive homes available. Then it occurred to me that ownership of the house Marla had refused to leave would immediately transfer to him—not that it ever hadn't been his. I wondered if he'd planned to take occupancy. Then I remembered that not only was he sitting in jail, but his ex-wife's blood was also still all over the floor.

I closed my eyes as the scene flashed back to me—Marla's inert body with a pool of blood underneath her and soaking into the carpet. There was no amount of stain remover that could take out that amount of blood.

I took a deep breath, glad for the salty crispness of the air and the breeze from the open-air cart. Kate shouted directions to Mack from the backseat, and he guided us around the perimeter of the island, slowing as we bumped over gravel. Finally, he turned into a driveway fronting a house that looked like a whitewashed conch shell standing on its end.

"They're staying here?"

We'd passed the house before, but it hadn't occurred to me that the distinctive property was for rent. Then again, knowing what little I did of Richard's wealthy former client, the ostentatious house made total sense.

"According to the information she gave me," Kate said as Mack powered down the cart, and the second cart carrying the rest of our crew skidded up next to us.

"These babies handle like they're on rails," Leatrice said as she hopped from the driver's seat.

I supposed that compared to her Ford Fairmont, most vehicles handled like a dream.

"You let her drive?" I said to Richard as he dismounted from the back on visibly shaky legs.

"She was already in the seat and about to drive off. It was either get in and hold on for dear life or stay home."

"Regretting your decision?"

He clutched my arm for balance. "More than you know, darling."

Kate peered at her phone as she strode past the stone wall. "She said to join her at the pool."

"Where's the pool?" Leatrice asked as she hurried up to join Kate.

They both paused after they rounded the stone barrier, and the rest of us walked up behind them to see a kidney-bean-shaped pool filled with sea green water.

"There's the pool," Kate said.

My stomach dropped as I saw what was floating face down in it. "And there's Victoria."

CHAPTER 24

"What a gorgeous pool—" Fern said, sweeping his gaze across the pool deck that was ornamented with artistic rock statuary and dotted with lounge chairs as white as the house. The words died on his lips as he sucked in a breath and staggered back. "Is that a body?"

"Taco Tuesdays!" Mack cried, and I suspected this was another of his location appropriate curses. He lumbered toward the water, followed in short order by Buster, and both men jumped into the pool.

I hated to tell my friends that the female floating in the water face down and with her blonde hair fanned out around her head looked beyond saving. Still, they splashed toward her, flipping her over and pulling her to the edge.

I knew we should leave the crime scene untouched, but I also knew they had to try to revive her. Part of me held out hope that she wasn't dead as Kate and I both hurried forward and helped roll her motionless body onto the pool deck.

Once she was on her back, I gasped and sat back hard on my heels. Her eyes were wide and glassy, and her skin was tinged blue. There wasn't even the smallest hint of life to her.

"She must have been in the water for a while," Leatrice said softly from behind us.

The puddle that retrieving her body had caused was spreading across the pavement and darkening the pale surface. Shaking my head, I stood and backed away before the water reached me.

"Maybe if we'd come sooner," Kate murmured as she remained by the body and water spread around her legs.

"Stop," I told her. "This isn't our fault. We came when she told us to come."

"It's the fault of whomever whacked her on the back of the head." Leatrice had walked around until she was standing near Victoria's head, and she pointed down at the blonde hair matted wet to the scalp.

I joined her, a sick feeling washing over me when I saw the gash at the crown of the woman's head. "She was hit over the head and then pushed into the water."

"Or she was hit and fell."

I bobbed my head numbly at Leatrice, still not quite able to believe that the woman who'd been so vibrant and friendly only hours earlier was now dead. Buster and Mack sloshed up the steps of the pool, their stance dejected as they made their way to us, more water sluicing off their leather clothes.

"There was no saving her." I put a hand on Mack's wet arm as he nodded with his chin trembling.

"Who would kill such a young girl?" Buster's voice cracked, and I wondered if he imagined their practically adopted daughter

Prue being in Victoria's place. The two twenty-somethings would have been around the same age.

"Someone who didn't want her to tell us what she knew." Leatrice pursed her bright-coral lips as she bent down on her haunches and studied the woman's lifeless face.

I turned away, unable to watch, and noticed Richard standing off to one side with his phone pressed to his ear. "Who are you calling?"

"The police, of course." He disconnected and took a shuddering breath. "This is a murder, and despite the fact that our crew trampled over the crime scene, the police should be allowed to do their job."

He was right, but I hated that the local authorities were going to find us at the scene of a murder—again. Like before, we alibied each other, but the optics weren't great. Victoria's death also put us right back to where we'd started when it came to narrowing suspects.

"Don't you have a call to make?" Richard gave me a pointed look.

It took me a moment to realize what and who he meant. "You want me to call Mike now?"

Richard touched the fingertips of one hand to his chest. "It's not me that wants you to call your husband. It's you who promised to tell him if anything suspicious happened again, and it's also you who assured him you were going to stay far away from even the faintest whiff of a crime."

I knew he was right, but I also knew what would happen the moment I called my husband and told him there had been a second murder. He'd be on the next flight down to whisk me home. It wasn't that I didn't want to see him, but I'd promised

Kate we would have a relaxing getaway to celebrate her before she got married. It would be a lie to say that the trip had been going according to plan, but the second Mike came down and whisked me away to safety, any chance of our celebration being saved was gone.

I had no intention of lying to him or even keeping the news from him for long, but I was also certain that I wasn't in any danger. Not when I was surrounded by Buster and Mack and had no connection to Mr. B.

I narrowed my eyes at him. "I didn't intend to walk in on a murder scene."

He opened his arms wide. "No one ever intends to walk into a murder scene, yet once again, here we all are."

"I hope you aren't implying that this is my fault."

"That you killed her, of course not. Don't be absurd, darling." He cut a brief glance at the body and looked just as quickly away. "I would like to point out that I wasn't a fan of believing this woman in the first place. I suspected she might not be telling the truth, and here we are."

I waved a hand in the general direction of the body. "It's not *her* fault that she's dead. She didn't exactly whack herself on the back of the head and throw herself into the pool. For all we know, she was telling the truth the entire time." I put my hands on my hips. "Actually, Victoria being killed proves that she did know valuable information, and someone wanted to silence her enough that they murdered her so she couldn't tell us."

Richard clamped his mouth so hard his lips became a white line. He knew I was right. Someone had a reason to want the woman dead, and the reason had to be that she knew something that could prove who killed Marla.

"We don't know that," Richard finally spluttered. "For all we know, there could be a serial killer loose on the island, and he's going after blondes."

Kate inhaled sharply. "What?"

"Richard's being ridiculous." I glanced swiftly at my friends around the body. "There's no serial killer on the island." Then I shot him a severe look. "A killer who only murders women married or engaged to your buddy?"

"He's not my buddy." Richard drew himself up and lifted his chin. "He's my client."

I squared my shoulders. "Former client."

"Um, Annabelle." Kate's voice trembled, and I tore my gaze from Richard to see her standing and staring behind us. I pivoted back to see the same police we'd met at Marla's house standing in the driveway. Well, this didn't look great.

"Who called us?" The uniformed man with the thick mustache stepped forward and took command. He also seemed to be the one with the best English.

Richard raised his hand. "That would be me."

The man's gaze slid from Richard to our friends huddled around Victoria. "Is that a dead body?"

"I did say on the phone that we'd found a woman floating in the pool."

"You did not say dead," the officer said, eyeing all of us with more suspicion as he walked forward.

Richard folded his arms over his chest and looked affronted. "I'm sure I said dead."

"She was dead when we arrived," I explained. "She was floating face down in the pool."

"You moved her?"

"We tried to save her," Kate said, her voice cracking.

The man nodded as he walked closer to Victoria, frowning as he retrieved a walkie-talkie from his waist and spoke rapid-fire Spanish into it.

"She didn't drown," Leatrice said once he was done. "At least, I don't think she did."

The man gave Leatrice and her Mexican peasant dress the once-over. "Why do you say that?"

Leatrice pointed to the gash on the woman's head. "She was hit on the back of the head. I'd guess that she was hit by someone and then pushed into the pool."

"Or she was pushed and fell," Fern offered.

"Either way, Mr. Bottinger had nothing to do with it," Richard said to me, no doubt intending for only me to hear him. "Which means the already weak theory of him being the killer is falling apart."

The officer spun around and pinned Richard with a shrewd look. "Why do you say he could have nothing to do with this?"

"Because he's in your jail," Richard said, clearly taken aback that the man had heard him.

"No, he's not. He was released an hour ago."

Richard emitted a high-pitched squeak as his knees buckled.

CHAPTER 25

"I'm fine." Richard waved away the second glass of water from Leatrice as he sat on the almost completely circular couch inside the seashell house. The room was as white as the exterior with a curved ceiling and walls, giving the feel of being inside a shell. The cushions we sat on were teal, but the throw pillows had images of coral in various shades of blue. I expected the room to smell of seawater, but instead my nose detected hints of lemon furniture polish.

"You don't look fine." She took a sip of the water herself and put it on the coffee table made from driftwood topped with a circular piece of glass. "You look like you just donated blood."

My observant neighbor was right. Richard looked like he'd lost several shades of skin tone, which was saying a lot since I was almost certain he'd been freshly spraytanned before our trip.

"Was it the shock of realizing that your client might actually be a cold-blooded killer?" Kate asked from the other end of the couch that was big enough to fit all of us.

"I can't believe he would commit murder," Richard said. "He and his fiancée seemed so happy when I saw them the other night."

"We don't know he did it." Fern glanced at the door where an officer was stationed on the other side as their team processed the crime scene. "Although it doesn't look good for him."

"There's literally no one else who could have done it," I said. "Who else on this island has motive to kill both women? Who else on this island knows both women?"

"Aside from us?" Fern tapped a finger on his chin, and his enormous ring caught the light from the sunset streaming through the round window behind us.

Richard moaned and put his head in his hands. "This is a disaster."

No one spoke. It wasn't a total disaster—all of us had alibis and no motive—but it wasn't going great.

"I've been on better vacations," Buster finally said, his voice rough and deep. He hadn't spoken much since he and Mack had pulled the body from the pool.

"We've also been on worse," Mack offered, shifting his weight so that his leather pants made a strange groaning sound. "There were more bodies in Bali."

"And our lives were in danger," Fern said with enthusiasm.

Leatrice released a sigh. "I wish I'd been on *that* trip."

"The beaches were beautiful," Kate said.

Fern nodded. "And there were golf carts, so not so different from this."

I held up my hands. "Let's not compare trips we've taken where bodies have piled up around us."

"I would like to hear about those trips."

We all whirled toward the doorway where the officer stood, stroking one finger down his mustache. I had to get better about listening for doors opening.

"It's nothing." I forced a laugh. "We were joking around."

He raised a brow at this but seemed to let it go. "Tell me why you were here."

We all swung our heads to Kate, whose cheeks flushed.

"She texted me." Kate held up her phone. "The victim, Victoria, that is. We'd met downtown, and she sent me a message later saying she needed to tell me something about Marla's murder."

Now the officer's eyes widened. "What did she tell you?"

"Nothing." Kate shook her head. "She wanted to meet in person to tell me. I got the feeling she didn't want to put it in writing. She sent me an address and told me a time. When we got here, she was already dead."

"And you saw no one else here? No one leaving? No car driving away?"

Why hadn't I thought of that? I frantically searched my memories for any of someone leaving the seashell house when we'd arrived but came up blank.

"No," Kate said. "I didn't notice anyone, and there was no car near us on the road when we drove up."

"There are plenty of other houses on this street though," Richard said. "Anyone could have run off and hidden in another yard."

Leatrice snapped her fingers. "Or run across the street and past those houses, and they'd be at the beach."

My shoulders slumped. "So, whoever did this could have gotten away pretty easily?"

"No one has gotten away with anything." The officer's expression was severe. "We are a small island and a small police force, but we will catch who did this." He swept his gaze over us. "You should return to your house."

Richard stood first. "I'm driving." Then he marched from the room without a backward glance.

I hurried after him, not sure if he intended to wait until he had a full golf cart to leave. I cut a glance to the pool area as we walked toward the driveway, flinching when I saw that they hadn't yet removed the body. It was covered with a sheet, but Victoria's form was still easy to make out lying in an evaporating puddle of water on the concrete.

"What about dinner?" I asked Richard as I slid into the passenger's seat of the nearest golf cart. Despite the horror of finding another dead body, I couldn't deny that I was still hungry.

"If ever there was a time for delivery," he said as he started the cart, "it was tonight."

Night had fallen since we'd been inside the house, and the sound of chirping insects filled the air. By now, downtown would be bustling with activity and the restaurants would be packed. Richard was right that we might not make the cheeriest dining party.

He jerked the cart into gear as Kate and Fern hopped on the back. "Let's see if we can avoid finding any more corpses if we stay in."

Kate grabbed the bar overhead to keep from flying off as Richard accelerated onto the road. "Well, now he's jinxed it."

Since the trip was starting to feel cursed, I hoped we wouldn't be adding a jinx to our growing pile of problems.

I closed my eyes for a moment and let the cool evening air blow on my face as we bumped along toward our house. The small room in the house had given me a sense of claustrophobia, and I was glad to be outside, even if it was dark.

When I opened my eyes, I glanced to my right at the graveyard across from the ocean. The whitewashed, aboveground graves shone bright in the moonlight along with the colorful flowers and icons adorning the tops. A few people were gathering at tombs of their family members, and surprisingly upbeat guitar music wafted in the breeze.

Just as I was about to face forward, I caught sight of something from the corner of my eye and my heart lurched. I whipped my head around in time to see the blonde in the wedding dress spin away from me and vanish behind a tall cross.

My pulse spiked as I tried to catch my breath and convince myself that I hadn't just seen the ghost of Marla walking among the graves.

CHAPTER 26

"You've been quiet." Kate padded barefoot into the living room as she rubbed the sleep from her eyes. Her pink satin eye mask printed with long bedazzled eyelashes was pushed to the top of her head and matched her silky pink shorty pjs. "You barely talked during dinner last night."

I wrapped my hands around my warm mug of herbal tea, wishing desperately that it was coffee augmented with lots of mocha and sugar. "Yesterday was a long day."

"I guess it was." She yawned and walked into the kitchen, surveying the Styrofoam take-out containers still strewn on the counter.

Even though I'd opened the sliding glass door to let in some morning air, the house still carried the aroma of Italian food. We'd had delivery from Ronaldi's, since it was the only take-out menu we could locate in the house, but everyone had drifted off to their rooms almost as soon as we'd eaten. I hadn't been the only one who'd been worn out from the day's misadventures, but I'd been the only one with a pregnancy and lack of a nap to blame it on.

For some reason, I hadn't wanted to mention what I'd seen—or thought I'd seen—the night before. We'd all been too on edge, and I'd been so weary I could barely keep my eyes open, much less debate the possibility that I'd actually seen the ghost of Marla.

Kate pulled a jug of orange juice from the fridge and poured herself a tall glass. Then she opened a Styrofoam container and grabbed a garlic knot, munching on it as she joined me on the other end of the couch.

I was surprised she didn't pour a few glugs of booze into her glass. "You're drinking that virgin?"

"After yesterday, I think I need to have a cleanse today."

I eyed the bread knot as she took a bite. "Your cleanse includes cold garlic bread?"

She swallowed and nodded. "It sure does." Then she pointed to the kitchen. "You want me to grab you one?"

I shook my head and held up my tea. "I'm good."

Kate took a sip of her juice and made a face. "It tastes so strange to drink it straight." My former assistant and new business partner tilted her head at me, the oversized eyelashes on her eye mask tipping to one side. "Are you sure you're good? You're not usually so quiet during murder investigations."

I shrugged. "To be honest, it feels different now that I'm pregnant. I'm not just making decisions for myself anymore. I used to think I was being careful and avoiding danger, but now I know I wasn't."

"Do you think we're in danger?"

I thought about that. When Marla had been killed, I didn't think we were in any danger because I'd assumed it was a crime of passion, and from what I'd seen of the woman, I had no problem imagining that there were many people passionate about seeing her dead. Even though the crime had taken place next door, I'd never felt unsafe. Even when we'd found Victoria dead in her pool, I'd never thought her death wasn't targeted and connected to Marla's. So, did I think one of us was a potential target by the same killer who'd eliminated the two women? No, but I would be lying if I said that poking into the crimes might not attract the killer's attention.

"I think we should be careful." I took a sip of my now lukewarm tea. "I was serious when I told Richard I couldn't be involved, but somehow I've gotten sucked in, anyway."

Kate's face fell. "That's my fault. I never should have agreed to meet Victoria. If we hadn't gone to the house, we wouldn't have found the body and be pulled further into the case."

"You didn't know she'd be dead, and we all made the decision to come with you."

"Because it was supposed to be a quick stop on the way to dinner." She sighed. "The best lame plans, right?"

"Best laid plans?" I couldn't help grinning at her word mix-up, which in this case, wasn't so inaccurate.

Kate glanced over her shoulder toward the closed bedroom doors. "You don't think Richard is still convinced his client is innocent, do you?"

It was a good question. Richard also hadn't been very talkative when we'd returned to the house the night before. I suspected he was dealing with the fact that Victoria's murder not long after Mr. Bottinger's release from jail did not bode well for the man. "I honestly don't know."

Kate leaned back on the couch cushions and tucked her feet under her. "I still can't believe someone killed that poor girl. She might have been a little crazy, but she seemed genuinely nice."

"Crazy?"

"You know." Kate circled a hand in the air. "The whole thing about her being convinced she was being haunted by Marla's ghost."

My breath caught in my throat, and my mug almost slipped from my hands.

"Whoa." Kate straightened and looked at me hard. "You look like you just saw a ghost."

I blew out a breath. "What if I told you that I might have?"

She swiveled her head around wildly. "Right now? Here?"

I shook my head. "Last night on the way back from finding Victoria." I flashed back to the drive back in the dark. "We drove past that cemetery, and I was sure I saw Marla—or someone who looked a lot like her—walking around the graves."

Kate's eyes were wide. "Creepy. How did you know it was her?"

"She was dressed in a white lace wedding dress, had the same blonde hair, and the identical skull makeup."

Now Kate's jaw dropped. "I'd say the wedding dress and makeup aren't too unique considering the Day of the Dead festival, but there aren't a ton of Mexican blondes."

"Especially not at the local graveyard. The only other people I noticed were locals hanging out at family graves."

Kate shivered. "You don't really think it was a ghost, do you?"

"No." I didn't, did I?

"If it's not a ghost, then there's a blonde running around in a lace wedding dress and skeleton makeup just like Marla was wearing when she was killed." Kate nodded her head as if agreeing with her own idea. "Which means that maybe Victoria wasn't crazy. Maybe she saw the same person you did and thought it was ghost. Maybe because she was too tipsy, or maybe because she also felt guilty about stealing Marla's husband and being the reason the woman was losing her husband and her house."

I liked the idea of a coincidence more than the possibility of a vengeful spirit back from the dead. "I guess it isn't a wild idea that more than one blonde would dress like a Day of the Dead bride and wear the full makeup. I mean, it is the time of year for it, right?"

Kate bobbed her head with enthusiasm. "Absolutely. There is zero chance that a murderous ghost bride is the one killing women on the island."

"I would hope not." Richard sounded scandalized as he walked from his bedroom into the living room. I was constantly amazed that his navy-blue pajamas looked as neat and pressed when he woke up as they did when he went to sleep. "Please tell me this isn't your new theory about the case."

"No theory," Kate said, smiling at him over the rim of her orange juice. "We were just coming up for reasonable explanations for the blonde in the wedding dress who looked just like Marla and was walking in the graveyard last night."

Richard stumbled over his own feet and caught himself on the back of a chair. "I beg your pardon?"

Kate jerked her thumb at me. "Victoria wasn't the only one to see someone who looks like Marla hanging around. Annabelle also saw her."

"When?" Richard gripped the back of the chair.

I gave him a curious look. "Last night on the drive back here, but why are you so worried? Kate and I have already determined that it was nothing. There might not be a lot of blondes running around in full Day of the Dead costume, but there must be some."

"Of course," Richard muttered. "That makes sense."

I sat up and stared at him. "Why are you so freaked out? You didn't even see her?"

He looked up and bit the edge of his lip. "Actually, I did. Just not last night."

CHAPTER 27

"You what?" Kate jerked up like she'd been given an electric jolt, and her eye mask popped off her head and sailed through the air to land on the tile floor.

Richard darted his gaze to the eye mask staring up at him and then back to us. "To be honest, I didn't think much of it at the time."

Kate narrowed her eyes. "What time was that? How long have you been hiding this?"

He squared his shoulders and let out an indignant huff. "I wasn't hiding anything. I merely didn't think it was notable." He flicked his fingers through his perfectly spiked hair that also did not look as if it had been slept on. "I also wasn't sure if I was imagining it or not."

I understood that, but I also wasn't sure what he was talking about. "Start from the beginning."

"Ooo, are we gossiping?" Fern asked as he stumbled from his room in a satin paisley robe that reached his ankles.

"Not gossip." Kate patted the space between us on the couch. "Richard is finally confessing that he also saw Marla's ghost."

Fern picked up his pace and plopped between us. "I love a good ghost story."

"I did not see a ghost." Richard scowled as he took the chair across from us. "I saw a blonde who looked shockingly like Marla in her wedding dress and skeleton makeup, but she was flesh and blood."

Fern's eyes grew wide. "There are multiple Marlas? How terrifying."

I couldn't argue with that. Multiple Marlas were terrifying, which was probably why Victoria was freaked out; why I was startled; and why Richard didn't even mention it.

"Richard was telling us when he had his Day of the Dead Marla sighting." Kate waved a hand at Richard for him to continue.

"It was the night of the festival." Richard rubbed a hand across his forehead, as if smoothing out the nonexistent wrinkles. "After the parade from the graveyard and the official celebration, we were all milling around. I'd already seen Marla in the crowd, but then I turned around and saw her again. For a second, I didn't know how she'd moved so quickly." A small shudder passed through him. "Then I realized it wasn't the same person."

Fern leaned forward and clutched the sides of his robe together at his throat. "How did you know?"

Richard hesitated for a beat. "Her hair was blonde, but it wasn't the same shade, and the cut was a bit different."

Fern nodded and made an approving noise in his throat. "I would have called Marla a buttered toast blonde. What shade was Marla number two—caramel, golden wheat, honey ginger, butterscotch, glazed apricot?"

"Buttered toast?" Kate cocked her head to one side then put a hand to her stomach. "I could go for some buttered toast."

The mention of so much food also made my stomach grumble. "Buttered toast does sound good."

Richard gave Fern a withering look. "You must have lost your mind if you think I know that many shades of blonde."

Fern shrugged. "But you're sure it wasn't the same shade?"

Richard gave him another look. "I've been catering for the Botoxed Blondes of DC for half of my life. I know the difference."

Fern held up his palms and sank against the back of the couch. "I believe you."

"What did you think when you saw the second Marla?" I asked.

"I didn't think I was seeing a ghost; I can tell you that much." Richard sniffed. "She was very much alive and walking around."

"But she looked enough like Marla that you did a double take?" I pressed.

Richard exhaled. "I did. For a second, I thought I was seeing double."

I swiveled my gaze around at my friends. "So, two of us have now seen this Marla look-alike."

"Don't forget Victoria." Kate held up a finger. "She saw her more than once."

"Three of us that we know," I corrected. "Do we really think that it's some coincidence? And why is this person continuing to dress this way. I know the Day of the Dead festivities last for several days, but I have a hard time imagining that a tourist is so into the traditions that they are dressing up for multiple days in a row."

"It might be different people," Kate said. "We can't know for sure that each of you didn't see an entirely different Marla."

"So, even more Marlas running around the island?" Fern made a face. "This story is getting scarier by the minute."

"I'm just saying that it might not be one person. There's a strong chance that there are a bunch of blonde tourists who have dressed in bride costumes at various points over the past few days, and each of you has seen a different one."

Richard pursed his lips and nodded. "That is the logical explanation."

Now that Kate explained it like that, my Marla sighting didn't seem so sinister, although at the time I'd absolutely been creeped out by it. Besides, who would have any reason to impersonate Marla?

"Now that we've solved that, I think it's time for some breakfast." Fern stood and rubbed his hands together. "I know it's time for coffee."

Kate slid her feet to the floor and stood, tossing back the last of her orange juice. "Are you cooking again?"

"No!" Richard called out before Fern could answer. "I'm handling breakfast this morning."

Fern swiveled around in place and blinked at him rapidly. "Are you saying you didn't like my huevos rancheros yesterday?"

"Nothing of the kind," Richard said, "but Annabelle has gotten some food sensitivities during her pregnancy, so I thought I'd make something she's guaranteed to keep down."

I opened my mouth indignantly. I hadn't had a hard time holding food down since my first trimester, not that the scent of fish or cigarette smoke didn't make me want to puke. Still, Richard made it sound like I was spewing every two minutes.

Then I recognized the look in his eyes. He was using me as an excuse so he could take over cooking duties, and we all stood a chance of getting a warm breakfast that didn't end up half on the floor.

Fern looked at me and pressed his hands to his cheeks. "I forgot all about your sensitivities. Are you also having strange cravings?"

I shot Richard a wicked smile. "I have been craving a sausage and green pepper pizza."

"Don't hold your breath for that, sweetie." Richard leveled his gaze at me. "I'm not Wolfgang Puck. I don't do pizza."

"We did have Italian last night," Kate said. "And I already had a cold garlic knot."

Richard grimaced as he stood and headed for the kitchen, pausing for a moment as he passed me. "I do have something to tell you after I finish making eggs Benedict."

My stomach rumbled at the thought of Richard's exquisite hollandaise sauce. "Something aside from your sighting of the second Marla? You're full of surprises this morning."

He mumbled something about not being good at keeping secrets as he continued into the kitchen and proceeded to sweep all the takeout containers into the trash.

"Did you hear that?" Kate asked over Richard's loud cleaning. She walked toward the door, and then I heard the knocking.

"Please don't let it be the cops," Fern said, working the satin belt of his robe in his hands. "I don't think I can take another murder."

"Why would it be the cops?" Kate asked as she threw open the door.

My husband and her fiancé were standing on the other side, suitcases behind them and serious looks on their faces.

My husband saw me and flashed me a dimpled smile he knew made my knees go weak. "Hey, babe."

"It's the hot cops!" Fern said, rushing forward. "Now it really is a bachelorette party!"

CHAPTER 28

"It's not that kind of bachelorette party," I told Fern once Mike and Daniel had come inside and pulled Kate and me into respective embraces.

"And we're not that kind of hot cops," my husband added when he released me from his hug long enough to glance over his shoulder at Fern.

"Your loss, sweetie." Fern gave him a knowing wink. "I always travel with a stash of ones on me."

I gaped at the hairdresser to the rich and infamous. "You do?"

He made a motion of zipping his lips. "You'll never know now."

"Is that who I think it is?" Richard emerged from the kitchen wearing an apron over his pajamas and oven mitts on his hands. When he saw the two Reese brothers, he let out a sigh of relief. "Thank heavens, you're here."

"Is this what you wanted to tell me later?" I asked Richard, who was avoiding my gaze.

He twitched one shoulder as he spun on his heel to return to the kitchen. "Maybe."

I pivoted back to Mike, leaning back and meeting his eyes, which had deepened from hazel to green since he'd swept me into his arms. "Did he call you?"

"I called him." Mike didn't look even slightly abashed. "After Sidney Allen talked to Leatrice. Once I heard there'd been another murder, Daniel and I agreed we should take a Mexican holiday."

"What about your case?"

"Solved it."

I gave him a playful smack on the chest. "Please tell me there isn't some patsy sitting in jail now because you needed to catch an early flight."

"Why do you think Sidney Allen isn't with us?" Daniel said in a low voice as he chuckled.

Kate erupted in a fit of giggles as she wrapped her arms around her fiancé's neck. "You're kidding, right?"

"Of course, he's kidding." Mike shot him a scolding look, even though his brother was the older one and usually the one to be more serious. "If we threw Sidney Allen in jail, we'd instantly become dog sitters."

"Did someone say dog?" Richard popped his head around the dividing wall. "I'm assuming Hermès is safe and sound back in DC?"

Mike gave him a thumbs-up. "Couldn't be safer or sounder."

Richard's shoulders sagged, and he vanished back into the kitchen.

"Hermès might or might not have participated in the neighborhood Halloween pet parade," my sometimes better half whispered.

"In costume?" I knew what Richard thought about animals in costumes, which was funny considering the number of designer accessories his Yorkie owned.

My husband ran a hand through his dark hair and one curl fell onto his forehead. "He was a taco."

I put my hand over my mouth to keep from laughing out loud.

"Leatrice bought it before she left so that Hermès could be with you all in spirit." Mike's mouth quivered at the corners as he stifled his own laughter. "I have to say, he looked quite dashing for a dog wrapped in a fabric tortilla."

"You can't tell Richard, or he'll never leave Hermès again."

Mike made a show of making an X over his heart. "Not a word."

I ran a hand down the side of his face. "As happy as I am to see you, it really wasn't necessary to fly all the way down here. I'm not in any danger."

He furrowed his brow. "I've heard that way too many times, and it's never been true." He put a hand over my belly. "Besides, I missed you both."

I covered his hand with mine as my stomach fluttered. "We missed you."

His pupils flared. "Did the baby just kick?"

I nodded, my cheeks warming at the sight of his excitement. "Either they know you're here or they're hungry."

"Have you been eating? Richard was supposed to make sure you ate, and not just chips and salsa."

"I have been eating, although I haven't said no to any chips and salsa."

Mike closed his eyes for a beat. "I could go for some chips and salsa. You know they don't feed you on planes anymore."

"The last food we had were a few packets of cookies," Daniel said, taking a deep breath. "But it smells amazing in here."

"Richard took over the chef duties," Fern said with a half shrug. "Apparently, we're going to be eating regular old American food from now on instead of the authentic cuisine I was cooking."

I would have hardly called Richard's food regular or American, but it would be hot and end up on plates instead of the floor and stove.

"Need help with your bags?"

Buster's deep voice was a rumble as he and Mack walked up from the driveway in their skeleton pajamas and plucked the suitcases from the doorstep and brought them inside.

Daniel's face registered shock. "Are you two just coming home?" He let his gaze travel down the black PJs that snugly encased the burly men. "And you wore that?"

Mack chuckled as he thumped Daniel on the back. "We're staying in the guesthouse. It's attached but has a separate entrance."

Mike leaned his mouth close to my ear. "I don't think the island is ready for Buster and Mack in body conscious sleepwear."

Daniel's jaw gaped slightly as he looked over Kate's head.

"Look who's here!" Leatrice screeched from behind me as she ran up in her matching body conscious skeleton PJs that bloused off her. She threw her arms around my husband from behind and then did the same to Daniel. She didn't look surprised, which told me that Richard wasn't the only one who knew they were coming.

Mack shoved the sleeves of his pajamas up to reveal his thick, tattooed forearms. "Did you just arrive?"

"Morning flight," Daniel grinned at Kate, who was beaming at him.

"Does this mean the bachelorette party is officially over?" Leatrice asked.

Fern put an arm around her shoulders. "Adding hot cops to a bachelorette party never means it's over, sweetie."

Leatrice grinned widely, although I was pretty sure she had no idea what Fern meant by that. At least, I hoped she didn't.

"He doesn't think we're going to strip, does he?" Mike asked me, worry crossing his face.

I cocked an eyebrow at him. "I guess that's the risk you take crashing a bachelorette party."

"I'll do a private showing." He flashed me another heart-melting smile.

My pulse quickened, and his grin widened. "The baby kicked again."

"I guess that's a yes to the private strip show."

The loud sound of a throat clearing made us all turn.

"If you want the eggs Benedict to not be a glutinous mass, I suggest you grab a plate," Richard said with a wave of his oven mitts as if he was directing air traffic.

We all proceeded to the kitchen where Richard began handing over plates filled with perfectly poached eggs covered in creamy Hollandaise sauce. I breathed in the savory aroma and fought the urge to dip my finger in the sauce.

"So," I said to Richard once he'd passed out the last plate and was pulling off his oven mitts, "I heard that you talked to Mike last night."

My husband had joined his brother and Kate on the couch, saving a spot for me, while I loitered at the kitchen island pinning my best friend with a look.

"I didn't call him," Richard said in his defense, before adding, "but I probably would have this morning."

My brows lifted in surprise at the honesty.

"I promised him I would make sure you were safe, and I realized after we found Victoria's body that I'd lost sight of that. I thought I could help Mr. Bottinger and regain some of my former glory working for him again, but I don't believe he's innocent like I used to. And if he's dangerous enough to kill his own fiancée, then being involved with him in any way isn't safe." His voice trembled. "I already apologized to Mike for losing my head, but I owe you an apology."

I was so gobsmacked that my mouth fell open as he looked up and met my gaze. He really thought he owed me an apology for getting caught up in an investigation.

A laugh burst from my lips. "You're apologizing to me after I've dragged you into multiple murder investigations?"

"Don't worry, Annabelle," he drawled. "The irony isn't lost on me."

I smiled at him and walked around the island stove to put my hand on his arm. "If anyone understands the overwhelming desire to fix things for a client—even a former one—it's me. I've lost my head more than once trying to prove someone's innocence."

"I know." His voice was deadpan. "I was there every time."

"You have been the person I was trying to prove innocent before," I reminded him, giving his arm a squeeze. "Why don't we call it even?"

He leaned over and gave me a peck on the cheek. "Gracious as always, darling." He cleared his throat and looked away. "Now you'd better eat up before the eggs are ruined. After Fern used about three dozen yesterday, I don't have any for do-overs, and baby Gerard needs his sustenance."

One more reason to be glad my husband had arrived. He could break it to Richard that the baby wasn't going to be named Gerard.

CHAPTER 29

"Are you sure you're up for this?" Mike asked as we stepped from his rental car onto the sidewalk. He'd insisted that driving me around in a golf cart was not safe, so he'd rented a compact car that had seen better days.

"I'm actually glad to leave the house." I breathed in the scent of frying churros as he walked around to my side of the car and took my hand. "The last time I got out, we ended up at the seashell house with a dead body."

"If I didn't know the whole story, I'd think you were talking in some kind of code."

Everyone had brought the Reese brothers up-to-date on the murders and the investigation—not that we were a part of that—while we'd eaten our eggs Benedict. For the most part, the men had remained quiet while we'd relayed the events of the past few days, but I knew both of their detective brains were working in overdrive.

"You have to have a margarita," Kate said as she and Daniel emerged from the backseat of the car.

DAY OF THE WED

Her fiancé laughed and glanced at his watch. "It isn't noon yet."

"It is somewhere." Kate grabbed his hand and tugged him toward the compact downtown where T-shirt stores and restaurants were already busy.

A group of people in bathing suits carrying fins and snorkels walked past us toward the water, their flip-flops smacking the hot pavement. It reminded me that we hadn't done much since we'd been on the island aside from eat, drink, and hang out in our pool. The island was known for its beautiful diving and snorkeling spots, along with excursions into deeper water to swim with whale sharks. Not that I thought my husband would think that was an appropriate activity for me.

"I know you came down here to keep me from getting into trouble," I said as Mike and I walked along hand in hand behind Kate and his brother, "but is there anything you want to do while you're here?"

"Aside from the private strip tease?"

My cheeks flamed with heat at his teasing tone, and I nudged him with my shoulder. "Yes, aside from that."

He drew in a deep breath. "I figured that keeping you and your crew out of trouble or out of jail would eat up most of my time, so it hadn't occurred to me that I would be able to do anything else."

I shot him what I hoped was a withering look. "Well, aren't you surprised that no one is a suspect or being held for questioning?"

"I am, actually." He grinned at me. "It's a refreshing change."

I fought back a laugh. "You act as if I spend most of my life one step away from being arrested for murder."

He slid his gaze to me but remained quiet.

"It's been a very long time since any of us were actual suspects," I said before thinking if that was actually true. It felt like it had been a while.

"I'm just glad this time it's different and the killer is already in custody."

"Is he?" The last I'd heard, Mr. Bottinger had been freed from jail thanks to his expensive and influential lawyer, but that had also been before his fiancée had been found murdered.

Mike nodded. "I talked to the local police before we arrived. I wanted to introduce myself, explain why I had an interest in the case, and let them know that Daniel and I would be arriving on the island."

"You did?" Despite his laid-back appearance, my husband had been busy.

"I wanted the cops in charge to know that you and your friends might seem guilty because you always end up in the wrong place at the wrong time, but that you're actually harmless."

Somehow, I didn't think harmless was the way he'd described us to the Mexican police, but I also didn't want to know how he portrayed my eclectic crew to fellow cops.

"It's a relief to know that the killer is behind bars, but I still don't understand why he did it."

"Crime of passion, right?" Kate asked, turning around as she continued to walk.

"I guess." Despite being glad that the case had been solved, I still didn't understand why Mr. Bottinger would kill his soon-to-be ex-wife if he wasn't in danger of losing his house. If his prenup was solid, then we were supposed to believe that he'd killed her to stop her from trashing his new fiancée's name?

For some reason, I didn't buy that, either. A man that wealthy would much rather make a payout than get his hands dirty with murder. I would bet that he'd paid a lot more money for a lot less before. And why kill his fiancée, whom he'd appeared to be genuinely enamored with when we'd seen him at the festival? I didn't have any doubt that he might tire of her in a few years, but I'd seen lots of new love, and he'd been a man in the early stages of infatuation. Would a man in love really be able to kill the object of his affection?

"If he was a sociopath," I murmured to myself as we passed a souvenir shop with spinning sun catchers twirling in the breeze.

"If who was a sociopath?" My husband eyed me as Kate and Daniel paused to look at some jewelry in a shop window.

I shook my head. "Nothing. I guess I can't stop thinking about the chief suspect. I'm not saying Richard was right to blindly believe him, but it's hard to wrap my head around the man's motives."

"Not if he's a rich sociopath used to getting what he wants."

"True," I admitted. Besides, who else would have had motive to kill both women, or even knew them both?

I swept a hand across my brow and cast a longing look at the wide-brimmed straw hats.

"Why don't we get you some water?" My husband steered me toward a restaurant with tables on the sidewalk shaded by red canvas umbrellas.

I didn't argue. The heat and humidity combined with the extra baby weight made me tire more quickly and get hot faster.

Mike asked a waiter for waters as he took the menus and pulled out my chair for me.

"Good." Kate flopped down on the other side of me. "I thought it was margarita time."

The waiter returned with four waters along with baskets of chips and bowls of salsa. I eagerly drained my water and reached for the chips. I might have eaten eggs Benedict less than an hour ago, but there was always room for chips, especially ones that were fresh and hot like these were.

My husband leaned in and wrapped an arm around the back of my chair. "Better?"

"Much," I told him with a grateful smile as Kate ordered margaritas for her and Daniel. "Don't feel like you can't drink just because I can't."

He shook his head. "I'm driving." He glanced at my belly. "And I'm on duty."

My stomach did a little flip as his deep voice made me melt with happiness.

"Don't we know him?" Kate asked, poking me on the arm and breaking my happy spell.

I followed her gaze to the bar of the restaurant where a man sat slumped over a highball glass. "I'm pretty sure everyone we know on the island is either at this table or back at the house."

"I don't know." Kate wrinkled her brow as she peered at him. "He looks really familiar."

I looked harder at the youngish guy in a polo and khaki shorts. He had sandy brown hair and clearly wasn't a local, but Kate was right. There was something about him that tickled something in the back of my brain. "Is he from DC?"

We'd planned so many weddings that there was a distinct possibility that the guy was one of our groomsmen or maybe even a member of a band or a cater waiter. But a little voice told me that I'd seen him recently.

He straightened and chugged the rest of his drink then waved down the female bartender. "How about another, doll?"

I jerked upright as Kate swung her head toward me. That voice. I'd heard that voice before and very recently.

"That's the guy Marla was yelling at," Kate said in a stage whisper that was more stage than whisper.

The man at the bar spun around, made eye contact with us, and his mouth dropped open. I guess he recognized us too. Before we could say anything else, he leaped from the barstool and started running for the exit.

"Stop!" Kate stood and waved an outstretched arm at him.

"He was arguing with the first victim before she was killed," I said to Mike, as he jumped up from the sidewalk table along with Daniel.

The guy had a head start though and was out the open door of the restaurant before my husband and brother-in-law could even start after him. Then he ran straight into the human wall of Buster, who grabbed him by the back of the shirt before he fell to the ground.

CHAPTER 30

"How did you do that?" I asked Buster as he and Mack stood behind the man who was now slumped in a chair at our table.

Buster's sizable arms were crossed over his chest, and he looked menacing as he glared down at the man he'd stopped. "I didn't do much. He did most of the work by running into me."

"But how are you here, and how did you know where to find us?" Kate asked. "I thought you two were going to hang out at the pool."

"We were." Mack shifted from one leg to the other, and his black leather pants groaned from the exertion. "But then Fern and Leatrice decided that she needed to go blonde again, so the house smells like hair dye."

"I'm surprised Richard isn't with you." I glanced behind them in case their heft had somehow hidden my slim friend.

"He's at the market," Mack said. "He claims that Fern has decimated our supplies, and that now there are two more men in our party, he needs to restock."

I turned my attention back to the man sitting between Mike and Daniel. His head was down, his shoulders sagged, and he truly looked like a man defeated.

"Who are you?" my husband asked, his voice instantly taking on the authoritarian tone he used in interrogations.

The man lifted his head. "Brent. Brent Harwood."

"You were the man arguing with Marla," I said, trying to sound less hostile so that I could be the good cop to Mike's scary cop.

He nodded, sliding his gaze between me and Kate. "I saw you two by the pool at the house next door. That house is usually empty."

"You and Marla were having an affair," Kate said. It wasn't a question because she knew. Being able to tell if people were involved by a mere glance was one of her superpowers, not that it would have been hard for anyone to tell they were dating. You didn't fight like that with someone you didn't care about.

Brent flinched at this. "It was more than an affair. We were in love."

From what the housekeeper had said, Marla had been involved with multiple men, although it didn't seem like Brent knew this. "You know she was married, right?"

He gave a half shrug. "She was getting divorced. The marriage had been over for a while."

Because her husband had left her for a younger model, I thought but didn't say. I doubted that was information Marla shared with her younger lover. I reached for a chip and dunked it in the salsa. Just because we'd cornered a new suspect didn't mean I wasn't still hungry.

"So why were you fighting that day?" Mike asked, pulling the man's attention back to him and making him jerk to attention.

Brent blew out a shaky breath and ran a hand through his hair. "It was stupid, but most of our fights were. Marla had a temper, and the divorce was making her crazy." He frowned. "Did you know her husband was trying to kick her out of her house? She'd put so much of herself into decorating it and—"

"The fight?" Daniel cut him off.

"Right." The man gave both Daniel and Mike an apologetic look. Then he snuck a glance behind him at Buster and Mack, who still stood with their arms crossed tightly over their chests, and he shuddered and turned back around. "Like I said, it was crazy. I thought she was sneaking around on me, and I asked her about it. She swore she wasn't and then said that I must have a guilty conscience because I was cheating on her."

That was a bit rich, considering that she was, according to Carlita, having multiple affairs while still married.

"Were you?" Mike asked.

Brent shook his head so hard his hair flopped into his eyes, and he had to swipe his bangs to one side. "Never. Marla and I were in love. She said that once she'd gotten her settlement and what she'd earned, we could get married."

I stared at the guy as his bottom lip quivered. Either he was the world's best actor, or he'd really loved the woman and believed every word she'd told him.

"Why did you think she was cheating on you?" Kate asked as she took a sip from her very full margarita.

Brent's gaze dropped to the hands he was clutching in his lap. "I saw her."

"Saw her...?" I prodded when he didn't say anything more.

He released a tortured breath. "I saw her with another man." He groaned and the words spilled from his mouth. "I work for a company that fixes pools. That's how I met Marla."

I fought the urge to roll my eyes. Had the blonde soon-to-be divorcee been sleeping with the pool boy? I eyed Kate's cocktail jealously. This occasion definitely called for a drink, but I'd have to settle for dealing with the craziness sober.

"We got a call to come out to a new house—a really fancy one. They asked for me personally, so I guess they'd heard I do good work." Brent continued. "When I got there, the bedroom window blinds were open, and I could see right inside." His breath hitched in his throat. "Marla was facing away, but I knew it was her because she was wearing the pink negligee I'd bought her. She was sleeping with the guy who owned that big house."

Kate and I exchanged a glance. That was rough. Part of me wondered if Marla had given Brent's name because she wanted him to see her. Some women liked to play power games, and Marla struck me as exactly that type.

"But she denied it?" Daniel asked, breaking the tension.

"Completely. That's why we fought." He swiped at his eyes. "I would have forgiven her, but she was enraged that I would accuse her. She claimed that her negligee was missing, and then she started ranting about the help stealing her things and told me she never wanted to see me again."

"Is that why you killed her?" my husband asked. "Because she humiliated you and broke things off?

The man jolted upright. "I didn't kill her! I left and didn't go back to the house. I was going to go back the next day and talk to her, but I knew Marla, and she needed some time to cool off." His shoulders sagged. "Then I heard she'd been killed." His expression darkened as he fisted his hands. "Her ex-husband should be glad he's in jail because if he wasn't, I'd..."

Mike and Daniel both cocked their heads at him, but the man just scowled.

"I didn't kill her. I loved her." He shook his head slowly. "I never should have confronted her and told her I saw her with that other man. Maybe if I hadn't, then I would have been with her in the house, and she wouldn't have been killed."

"Can you prove you weren't at her house when she was killed?" Mike asked.

Luckily, Brent hadn't thought to question who Mike and Daniel were or if they had any authority to question him. Then again, they exuded command and two burly leather-clad men who looked like Hell's Angels were guarding him. He had no way of knowing that they were born-again Christian bikers who wouldn't even curse.

Brent bobbed his head up and down. "I was in the drunk tank at the jail. I drowned my sorrows about Marla breaking up with me a little too much and ended up making a scene and getting thrown in jail to sleep it off."

Mike glanced at me. It would be easy enough to check, but I knew from his expression that he was thinking the same thing I was. The guy was innocent. Which meant there were still no other decent suspects aside from the one sitting in jail.

Then I remembered something else.

"You said you didn't go back to Marla's house after you fought that evening? Not even later that night?"

He furrowed his brow in confusion. "Later that night? I haven't been back to Marla's house since she ordered me out before the Day of the Dead festival."

That meant there was still one mystery man unaccounted for— the one I'd only seen in shadows.

CHAPTER 31

"I know that look." My husband narrowed his eyes at me as we watched Brent return to the bar and his drink. "I can practically hear the gears turning in your head."

"If Brent truly didn't return to her house that night—and he couldn't if he'd already been thrown in the drunk tank—then there's another man who was with Marla." I rested my hands on my belly and drummed them lightly. "It had to have been her ex, right?" I shook my head in frustration. "But why would he be at the house and argue with her and then leave and come back in the morning to kill her? I know she was alive earlier in the evening, because I saw her through the glass of her house."

"Unless who you saw was her ghost," Kate said with a laugh.

"Very funny." I shot her a look then froze. "Wait, what if it was the ghost?"

Kate's gaze shifted from me to Mike and back. "I thought you didn't believe that Marla's ghost was haunting people."

"I don't, but there have been a lot of sightings of a woman who looks so much like the deceased that everyone who saw her believed it was Marla—or if they believed in haunting—her ghost. What if one person was impersonating Marla to confuse things?"

"Seeing a dead woman is pretty confusing," Buster said from where he still stood with his arms crossed.

"Which is why I assumed I was seeing Marla when I spotted a blonde in a lace wedding dress in her house. But what if I was seeing someone pretending to be her when she was already dead?"

My husband nodded slowly as he digested this theory. "You did say that the blood had already soaked into the carpet when you saw the body, but that it couldn't have been more than half an hour since you'd seen her alive."

I pointed a finger at him. "Exactly. I knew something about the crime scene bothered me when we snuck over to the house."

"You snuck over—?" Mike started to say but I waved off his concern.

"Then that means the man I saw late at night could have been the one who killed Marla."

Kate wrinkled her nose. "That means the body would have been lying on the floor for hours."

I sagged in my chair. "Then the timing wouldn't be right. Marla didn't look like she'd been dead for hours when we saw her, and the blood would have been practically dried." It was hard to hide the disappointment in my voice. "So, the mystery man probably wasn't the killer."

"Maybe not," Daniel leaned forward, "but your theory about the woman dressed as Marla is sound."

Kate threw her hands up. "What woman wants her dead aside from maybe Victoria, and she ended up being murdered herself?"

"There's always Carlita," Mack suggested hesitantly. "She did find the body, and we're just taking her word for that."

"We know she didn't like working for the woman, but I can't imagine she'd murder one of her paying clients," I said.

Kate shook her head to agree with me. "And rush over hysterically to tell us? You can't fake panic like that."

"So, if Carlita is out and Victoria is dead, what other woman on the island had a motive to kill her?" Mack asked, glancing around as if the killer might leap out from a dark corner.

I released a loud breath. "None that we know of, which means we're back at square one with a mystery man in the house at night and Mr. B as the number one suspect for both murders."

Kate took a sip of her drink. "Richard will not be happy."

"There's another man we don't know much about," Daniel said, scratching the salt and pepper scruff on his cheeks.

Buster and Mack both leaned forward. "Who?"

"Who was the man that Brent saw with Marla? He said he was called to a fancy house and saw Marla in a compromising position with some man. Who was the man?"

I sucked in a breath. Of course. We hadn't even thought about that mystery man.

"Marla did deny that was her," Kate reminded us, then immediately gave a half shrug. "Not that we should take her word. It's not like the woman was known for her scruples."

"I think we have to assume she was lying for the purpose of turning over every stone in the investigation," I said.

My husband gave me a quelling look. "Not that you should be turning over any stones at all."

I put a hand on my chest and attempted to manufacture the false outrage I'd seen Richard and Fern produce on a daily basis. "I can't believe you would suggest…" I gave up when I saw the disbelieving look from Mike. "Fine, but just because I can't turn over stones doesn't mean someone else shouldn't." I pinged a look between him and Daniel. "We do have two DC police detectives at our disposal."

Daniel held up a finger. "Former detective."

I shrugged. "Once a cop…"

My husband sighed but glanced at the bar where the former object of our interrogation sat nursing a cocktail. "I guess it wouldn't hurt to find out more about the house belonging to the mystery man."

Excitement made my heart beat faster. "And I'll bet if we find the mystery man, we just might find the person I saw fighting with Marla the night she was killed."

Mike stood and walked toward the bar, giving me a backward glance that told me he was doing this for me.

Daniel released a sigh. "I guess this means I'm not going to see a beach today."

Kate perked up. "It doesn't take a village to track down one mystery man. I'm up for the beach."

"I wouldn't mind a walk on the beach," Buster said, which was a surprise considering I couldn't imagine it was fun to get sand stuck to black leather.

Mike returned to our table holding a cocktail napkin adorned with a red sombrero and some writing in black pen. "I have directions to the unknown man's house."

I took the napkin and peered at the messy writing. "I think I know which house this is, and he's right that it's fancy. It might be the largest one I've seen on the island." My hand trembled as I held the napkin and thought about how close we were to finding another piece to the puzzle. "And it's not far from our house—and Marla's."

"I'm in." Fern stood and started striding from the restaurant.

"Where are you going?" I called after him.

"Who are you kidding, sweetie?" He paused and gave me a wink. "You and your hot cop are obviously going to see the house, and I'm coming with you."

Mike grabbed my hand and pulled me up. "I guess we'd better go before he calls—"

"Shotgun!"

CHAPTER 32

"This is pretty swanky." Fern poked his head between the two front seats as we drove through a stone fence and past an open wrought iron gate to a spectacular house with a circular drive. Despite calling shotgun, he'd decided that sticking the pregnant lady in the backseat was bad form, especially since her imposing cop husband was driving.

I leaned forward to take in the impressive house that seemed to be all glass and sleek, white walls perched on a bluff overlooking the ocean. While most houses on the small Mexican island were built to resemble classic Mexican homes with thatched roofs and red tile—the seashell house being the notable exception—this house looked like it had stepped directly from the pages of Architectural Digest. It soared into the blue, cloudless sky, all sharp angles and sparkling glass.

Mike brought the car to a stop, and as we got out, I noticed that there were no other cars in the drive. There might have been a garage around the side of the house, but I couldn't see it.

We walked up to the front door and right by a massive master suite that stretched along one side of the house from the front to the back terrace that opened out to the pool deck. "I get how you could accidentally get an eyeful."

Fern wrinkled his nose. "I don't care how in the moment you are, a gentleman always closes the blinds."

I couldn't argue with that, but then again, voyeurism wasn't my thing. Marla might have been the type who liked to flaunt her conquests. Either that, or her mystery man did.

As we stood in front of the large, frosted glass door, my phone vibrated in my bag. "Sorry," I said as Mike pressed the doorbell, and I dug around in my purse.

I answered after glancing at the screen and braced myself for what I knew was coming.

"Where are you?" Richard shrieked through the phone. "You said you were going into town for a brief walk around, but now you're on the far end of the island."

I opened my mouth to explain, but then paused. "Are you tracking me?"

"Of course, I am." He let out an impatient huff. "You don't think your husband would have let you travel abroad without me promising to keep a very close eye on you, do you?"

"This was Mike's idea?" I slid my gaze to my husband's back and watched him tense when he heard his name.

"Who do you think taught me and installed the app on my phone?"

"You don't say?" I tapped my toe on the stone landing in front of the house, although I shouldn't have been surprised. My husband had made no secret of his attempts to keep me from going rogue.

"You haven't answered my question, Annabelle." Richard's tone had gone from impatient to irritated. "Why are you at some random spot in the middle of nowhere?"

"It's not random." I lowered my voice, even though there were no signs of movement within the house after Mike had rung the bell twice. "We're at the house where Marla's boy toy saw her in bed with another man."

"What?" Richard spluttered. "Boy toy? Who is Marla's boy toy?"

Now I was the impatient one. "While we were downtown, we ran into the guy we saw arguing with Marla. He admitted that he was dating Marla but that she'd ended it because he'd seen her with another man and had confronted her."

Richard sucked in a sharp breath. "It's even more tawdry than we knew."

"Is he jealous he decided to stay at the house and catch up on work?" Fern asked in a loud whisper.

I quickly talked over Fern so Richard wouldn't have the chance to snap back. "Luckily, the guy remembered the house where he'd seen Marla with the other man, so we're here to see if maybe he was the mystery man I saw her arguing with the night she was murdered."

"Please tell me it isn't just you and Fern, and yes, I could hear every word he said."

"It's not. Mike is here. Coming here was his idea."

My husband gave me a look that told me that was a stretch.

"Then I'm on my way," Richard said before the call disconnected.

Great. I dropped my phone back into my bag. Richard's nearly constant state of hysteria was just what we needed to question a potential suspect.

"No luck." Mike pivoted away from the door. "I guess we'll have to come back at another time."

"I'll bet the view from the pool is stunning," Fern said from where he'd wandered down the stone steps and around to the side of the house.

"Don't even think about…" My words were lost on him as he vanished around the corner.

My husband muttered a series of curses I hoped he'd remember not to use around our baby and then stomped off in Fern's footsteps.

"We're following him?" I asked as I hurried behind Mike.

"We're stopping him from doing something even more foolish that going around the back of the house."

He had a good point. There was a decent chance we were going to round the corner and find Fern floating in the pool on an inflatable swan.

The wrought iron gate that surrounded the back of the house stood slightly ajar, so we pushed it open and walked along a stone pathway to a perfectly manicured lawn that surrounded a breathtaking infinity pool that stretched toward the sea. Beige lounge chairs were positioned around the rectangular pool with open umbrellas shading them.

I didn't see Fern, and my pulse spiked. "Fern, where are you?"

"Here."

I spun around to see him standing at the back sliding glass doors and peering inside. My breath evened out, although I wasn't wild about him peering into the house. "We should go before someone finds us and calls the cops."

"What about this?" Fern pointed a finger at the glass, and I followed his gaze past the sliding door and into the expansive room that was filled with white-and-chrome furniture. I was about to tell him that just because the furnishings were obviously expensive didn't mean we should be staring inside. Then my eyes locked on the enormous painting over the modern inset fireplace.

"Is that…?" My husband asked, his mouth agape.

I nodded, unable to wrench my eyes from the painting of the blonde. "That's Marla."

CHAPTER 33

"Her lover was right," Fern said in a hushed tone. "Marla must have been having an affair with this guy. You don't put a woman on the wall if you're not—"

"Agreed," I said, stepping closer to the glass and squinting.

Mike shifted from one foot to the other. "Even if you are..."

The thought of us having a giant oil painting of me in our living room made a giggle escape my lips. "So that's a no on a wall-sized painting of me?"

He slid a bemused look at me. "Where would we put it?"

I was pretty sure our Georgetown apartment didn't have a wall as large as the painting hanging in this house.

"Are those genuine Jeanneret chairs?" Fern asked no one in particular as he pressed his nose to the glass. "They look vintage."

I wasn't up on my high-end furniture, but the entire place reeked of wealth. Whoever the mystery man was, he was clearly loaded.

As Fern leaned on the glass door, it slid to one side. He jumped back, swiveling his head and grinning at us. "It's open."

"Do not—" I stared to say as he pulled the door open the rest of the way and stepped inside the house.

"I just want to check out the chairs," he said with a causal wave at us.

I nervously looked around for any signs of movement inside the house or on the grounds. "Get back here!"

Mike took a few steps back. "Maybe we should wait at the car—"

"This isn't Marla," Fern called out from inside.

We both swung our heads to him and the open sliding door. Fern stood inside the house's large main room surrounded by the modern chairs and a glass coffee table as he peered up at the painting. I followed his line of sight to the blonde in the enormous painting. What was he talking about?

Fern craned his neck and beckoned for us to come inside. "I'm telling you, it isn't her. It looks a lot like her, but I know blondes. Marla was a buttered toast blonde, and this woman is a butter*scotch* blonde. Also, the eyes are different."

"It's a painting, not a photo," I whispered through the opening in the door. "It isn't an exact likeness."

Fern put his hands on his hips. "I'm telling you, this isn't Marla."

Now that I wasn't looking through glass at the image, I could see it without the reflection. I inhaled sharply. Fern was right. It looked a bit like Marla in the sense that the woman in the portrait was a blonde with the same hairstyle, but the faces weren't a match. I didn't know about the shades of blonde, but I was starting to think my friend was right.

"This doesn't make sense." I tightened my ponytail. "If that isn't Marla, then why does the man she's sleeping around with have a giant portrait of a woman that looks like her?"

"You don't think that's a painting of the victim?" Mike asked me.

I shook my head. "Fern is right. It could be a very bad likeness, but I don't think that's her."

"Very strange," he muttered as we stood side by side at the open glass door.

"I wonder who lives here," Fern said absently as he started walking from the main room.

"Where are you…?" My words died on my lips as Fern vanished from sight. "And he's gone."

My husband turned to me. "You want to follow him, don't you?"

I hated to admit that if he wasn't by my side, I would have already been inside the house and snooping around with Fern. More than once, I'd gotten stuck in awkward situations snooping around looking for clues, so I should have known better, but he was right. Every fiber in my being was itching to follow Fern and find out exactly who lived in this house. "I know it's wrong to go in."

He choked back a laugh. "That's reassuring."

The sound of a motor reached my ears, but from where we were standing, I couldn't see if it was the owner of the house arriving or Richard pulling up in a golf cart. It seemed soon for Richard to have gotten here, which meant that whoever owned the house might walk through the front door at any moment.

"Fern!" I half whispered, half yelled. "We've got company."

There was no reply from inside the house as my stomach did strange somersaults I didn't know were my nerves or the baby. "Should we make a run for it?" I cut my eyes left and right as I realized we were standing outside a wall of glass. "Or at least hide?"

Just as I was about to make a dash for the pristinely shaped bushes to the side of the house, Fern walked back into the main room smiling.

"Hurry," I waved an arm to make him walk faster. "We heard someone drive up."

Fern glanced over his shoulder but didn't pick up the pace. "Okay, but should I bring these?" He held up a blonde wig and what looked like a white lace dress. "I found them in the bedroom."

Time seemed to slow as I locked onto the two items in his hands and things started to shift around in my brain and fall into place.

"I think those belong to me."

CHAPTER 34

My gaze swung to the voice and my breath caught in my throat at the woman standing behind Fern on the marble steps leading down to the sunken living room. Then my gaze snapped to the portrait on the wall.

She was the blonde in the painting, not Marla. But there was no denying that the two women shared a lot of similarities, although this blonde was notably older, and her ash blonde hair looked like it hid a decent amount of gray. I suspected the painting was made many years earlier.

Fern hadn't moved from his spot, although he had twisted his head to lock eyes with the woman. I could see when he made the connection between her and the painting, and his mouth fell open.

Her gaze dropped to the wig and dress in his hands, and her eyes narrowed at Fern. "Who are you, and what are you doing with my things?"

Fern held up the items, his hands trembling. "These are yours?"

She put her hands on her hips without deigning to give him an answer. "You're in my house."

I couldn't help taking in the luxurious house with new eyes. If this was her house, what was she doing with a blonde wig and dress that would have made for an excellent Marla disguise? I suspected we were looking at the ghost of Marla who'd been spotted all over the island, but why?

"We should go," my husband said in a voice so low it was meant only for me, "and quickly."

Fern cocked his head at the woman as he took a few steps in our direction. "Have I done your hair before?"

"Fern!" Was he insane? Now was not the time to drum up business or give unsolicited advice on shades of blonde. Not when he was standing inside a stranger's home holding their belongings.

He cast a quick glance over his shoulder at me. "I've seen her before, and not running around in these." He held up the wig and dress.

"Mrs. Bottinger?"

Now Mike and I whirled in the other direction to see Richard standing behind us and staring inside. And behind him, wearing a colorful "After This We're Getting Tacos" T-shirt belted as a dress, was Leatrice.

Even though Richard rarely lowered the temperature in a tense situation, and Leatrice looked like she was bursting with excitement, I was grateful to see them both. "That's not Marla." I motioned my head toward the painting. "It only looks a lot like her."

"No." His eyes never left the well-preserved blonde. "Not the second Mrs. Bottinger—the first. That's Regina Bottinger, my old client."

"Richard?" The woman took a few steps forward, closing the distance between her and Fern. "Is that really you?"

I ping-ponged my head between Richard and the first Mrs. Bottinger as questions swirled in my head.

"It's been a long time," the woman said with a warm smile, as if we all weren't in a supremely awkward situation, and Fern might or might not have broken several laws. "I hope your business is still successful. I do so miss your delicious dinners."

Richard preened from the compliment, touching a hand to his chest. "It hasn't been the same without you."

I shot him a look. This was not the time for exchanging pleasantries with a former client, especially since said past client might very well be involved in her successor's death.

Richard had the good sense to appear mollified, and his gaze went to Fern, who was slowly moving closer to the door. He registered the items in Fern's hands, and he drew in a quick breath. Leatrice's brightly lipsticked mouth made a perfect O as she looked from the wig and dress to the blonde to the painting.

"I do wish you hadn't come here today of all days," the first Mrs. Bottinger said, her smile slipping.

"Is there something you want to tell me?" Richard asked, managing to keep his own voice conversational. "You know I'm the soul of discretion."

The woman let out a weary sigh. "Oh, Richard. I do miss our chats in the kitchen before the fabulous dinner parties I would throw for Victor's clients. If only all that hadn't come to such a cruel end."

Fern sidled closer, sliding his feet so that he appeared to glide across the glossy floor, but Regina Bottinger didn't seem to notice. Her gaze was far away as she talked about her past life in DC

"It was terribly unfair what happened." Richard made a disapproving sound in the back of his throat. "But she never replaced you. Not really."

"You're sweet to say so, but that conniving witch took everything from me." She curled her French tipped fingers into fists. "If it wasn't for her, I'd still be throwing the most stylish parties in Washington, and you'd be catering them for me."

"Those were the days." Richard let out a sad sigh of his own. "You know, I don't blame you one bit for wanting to get your revenge on Marla."

Her eyes went wide. "You don't?"

Richard shook his head and stepped forward, pushing me behind him and giving me a backward shove toward the driveway. "Not one bit. If you ask me, she finally got what she deserved."

The woman's shoulders sagged as she choked back a sob. "She did, didn't she?"

"It must have felt so good to kill her." Richard rubbed his hands together with barely repressed glee. "After everything she'd taken from you."

The original Mrs. B bobbed her head. "You know, I originally wanted to poison her, but the woman never finished a drink."

I remembered all the half-drunk glasses in Marla's house and on the tables around her pool. If you had to rely on the woman to drink poison from a cocktail, you'd be waiting a very long time.

"When I saw her alive and well at the Day of the Dead festival, I knew my poisoned tequila hadn't worked." The woman's lips went thin. "So, I came to her house to finish the job personally."

"Dressed as her," I said before I could stop myself.

"I waited until one of her lovers left in a huff, then I snuck up on her when she thought I was him returning to grovel." She shrugged. "Then I waited until morning to stage an argument on the phone so her neighbors would see her and called my darling ex-husband to come over. People always said Marla and I sounded alike, and when I told Victor that I, Marla, was willing to sign his divorce papers, he didn't question it."

"Clever," Richard said. "Get rid of Marla and frame your unfaithful ex."

She shrugged. "I've always been a multitasker."

"I remember that about you," Richard said in his most placating voice. "But why continue to impersonate Marla?"

The first Mrs. B giggled as if she was sharing a delicious secret. "That was just a bit of fun. I wanted to torment Victor's new side piece a bit."

Fern had stopped, apparently riveted by the confession.

"Until you found out she wasn't just a side piece," Richard said.

The woman's delighted expression faded. "Can you believe he was going to marry her? She was young enough to be his daughter—his granddaughter, even." She gave a vicious shake of her head. "I couldn't have another woman moving into my houses."

"So, you killed her?"

She glanced up at Richard, her face guileless. "I didn't mean to kill her. I went over to tell her the kind of man she was marrying. I thought if I warned her off, she'd leave him."

"But she didn't," Leatrice said in a near whisper.

The blonde's gaze shifted to her and then to Fern, and the dazed look on her face vanished. "No. The silly girl insisted that she'd stick by him." She walked to one side, disappearing behind a tall, white wall and emerging moments later with a gleaming chef's knife. "She was just as foolish as you all were to come here."

With a quickness startling for an older woman, she dashed for Fern and raised the knife over her head. Fern screamed and bolted for the open sliding door.

Mike pushed me behind him, blocking me with his body as Fern waved the wig and dress over his head and ran from the house, his blood-curdling screams piercing the air. Richard rushed to me, wedging his body between mine and Mike's as we all backed up, almost tripping over each other's feet. Leatrice seemed to be frozen in place, so Richard ran over in a huff and yanked her to the rest of us.

Fern was racing around the long, rectangular infinity pool, dancing precariously along the narrow lawn between the pool and the drop-off to the ocean, and the original Mrs. B was chasing after him, screaming that she wanted her wig and dress back. Fern seemed too terrified to realize that he still had the items in his hands, as he flailed his arms over his head as he ran.

Mike spun around and locked eyes with Richard. "Get her to the car."

He ran toward the chase, while Richard gave me a shove toward the driveway.

"If you think I'm leaving my husband with a knife-wielding killer, *you've* lost your mind," I told him as I planted my feet in the lawn.

Richard opened his mouth to snap back, but just then a golf cart skidded to a stop in the circular drive and Daniel, Kate, Buster, and Mack spilled out and ran toward us in various stages of beach attire. I'd never seen Speedos paired with leather, but I'd take any kind of cavalry.

CHAPTER 35

"Who is that?" Kate yelled as she raced up to me and Richard. She was in a pink-and-white striped bikini and had sunglasses pushed up to the top of her head.

In the race around the pool, Fern was in the lead with the blonde behind him slashing her knife up and down. Mike was running behind her, but he was keeping some distance between himself and the deranged woman.

"Mrs. Bottinger," Richard said, holding up a hand when Kate's eyes bugged out of her head. "The first one, my old client."

"The original Mrs. B lives here too?" Kate rubbed the heel of one hand across her forehead. "I thought this was a tiny, secluded island, but it seems like half of the rich divas in DC are here. We could almost start a satellite office."

Richard's brows peaked, and I glowered at him. "Don't even think about it."

Daniel was wearing black swim trunks and a T-shirt as he ran toward the pool, but it was Buster and Mack who made my mouth gape. They were both in brightly colored Speedos topped with their black leather biker vests, which made them look like Hell's Angels at a Pride parade.

"How are you here?" I asked Kate over Fern's screeching and Mrs. B's hurled threats.

She held up her phone. "You accidentally butt dialed me. I heard everything." She bobbled her head from side to side. "Well, a muffled version of everything, but enough to know you needed help." She glanced at Leatrice's makeshift taco-themed dress. "Nice shirt."

"But how did you find us?" I asked before Leatrice could launch into a story about the shirt.

Kate cut her eyes quickly to Richard. "He's not the only one who's tracking you, boss."

I tried to be outraged that seemingly all my friends were monitoring my movements, but it was hard to be angry when I was so glad they were there.

Richard tugged at my arm. "We still need to get you to the car and away from here."

I waved a hand at the chase in progress. "I'm not leaving Mike—or Fern."

By this point, the three additional men had reached the race around the pool. Regina Bottinger saw them, and her face registered shock and then rage.

"More usurpers!" She broke off chasing Fern and made a beeline for Buster and Mack.

The two burly florists were big, but they weren't especially fast. Mack ran for the pool loungers, pushing them in the woman's path. She screamed louder as she dodged them and dashed around the overturned furniture.

Fern ran up to us, heaving in breath desperately as he leaned over at the waist. "For an old biddy, she can run." He managed to smile at Leatrice. "Not that you're an old biddy, doll."

Leatrice giggled and fluttered a hand at him, the wrinkled skin on her arm jiggling. "Age is a state of mind."

Mrs. Bottinger froze in her pursuit of Mack and spun around. "Did you call me old?"

"And her hearing is great, too." Kate grabbed my elbow and jerked me with her away from Fern as the blonde resumed her pursuit of him and ran right toward us.

Fern threw his arms up again and screeched, sprinting for the house as all the men gave chase behind the impressively fast woman. I instinctively curled my arms around my belly and allowed Kate and Richard to shuffle me farther away from her.

Fern tore through the open sliding glass door with the knife-wielding woman close on his heels. Her face was flushed red, and her hair was hanging sweaty and limp in her face as she sucked in breath but didn't slow down. It was like she was a woman possessed, which at this point, I wasn't eliminating as a possibility.

Fern leapt over a pristine white couch while Mrs. Bottinger hurried around the back of it. Fern hurled one of the designer chairs he'd been admiring earlier at her, and she had to duck low to avoid being hit by it. This seemed to enrage her even more, and her eyes were wild as she shot back up.

"Holy guacamole!" Fern cried as he bounded over the glass coffee table and ran back out through the sliding door, pulling it shut behind him at the last minute.

He practically ran into the men giving chase, but deftly sidestepped them as they all headed for the killer barreling toward them. I drew in a quick breath as I saw what was about to happen, turning away as the blonde crashed through the glass door. The sound of shattering glass and her agonized screams made me cringe, and I looked back in time to see her lying on the paving stones outside the glass door that was no longer there.

Fern had slowed to a walk, and he sank onto the lawn as he realized that his pursuer was no longer chasing him. He flopped onto his back with his arms stretched over his head, his chest rising and falling quickly.

Daniel and Mike were huddled over the inert woman as Mike talked furtively into his phone, and Buster and Mack stood over them with their arms folded like sentries in case the murderous woman decided to rise again.

I ran over to Fern with Kate and Richard flanking me and Leatrice bringing up the rear. We all knelt beside him as he gasped for breath.

"That's it." He held up a finger as if making a pronouncement. "No more age-challenged blondes. They're too crazy." Then his gaze slid to Leatrice. "Except you, sweetie. You're perfection as a blonde." Then his eyes rolled back in his head, and he passed out cold.

CHAPTER 36

"How's he feeling?" My husband came up to me as Leatrice and Kate were fussing over Fern, who was now lying on one of the pool loungers that had been righted.

"Better." I leaned into my husband as he wrapped an arm around my waist. I took a moment to breathe in the salty sea air and relish the fact that I could hear the seagulls and the waves rolling into the shore now that people weren't running around screaming bloody murder. "He's decided not to take out his recent experience on all his aging blonde clients."

"On a probationary basis only." Fern sat up slightly. "I still think all that bleach might make them crazy."

Leatrice patted his arm and pushed him back down. "You'll feel better after some rest and relaxation."

"Which this vacation has been very short on." Kate glanced back at me.

I held up my hands. "Don't look at me. I wasn't the one who wanted to get involved in the case."

"For once," she said under her breath.

"I think we should all be glad that I didn't ignore my gut feeling about Mr. Bottinger." Richard walked up to us and flicked his fingers through his spiked hair.

"What about your gut feeling about his deranged ex-wife?" Fern sat up again and waved a hand in the direction of the woman being loaded onto a gurney and surrounded by local police. "That didn't really work out, did it?"

Richard put his hands on his hips. "How was I supposed to know that my client from ages ago had an unhealthy obsession with her ex-husband's new wife?"

"Wives," Mike corrected. "She killed both of them."

Richard slid a wounded gaze to him. "Et tu, Brutus?"

Leatrice perked up. "Oh, are we finally using code names?" She swept a hand across the sky as if painting across it. "I've always wanted my alias to be The Icy Cold Hand of Death."

"Subtle," Richard drawled. "It really trips off the tongue."

I shot him a look before bursting my neighbor's bubble. "No code names."

She frowned, but immediately brightened when Buster and Mack joined us, along with Daniel. "At least the gang is all here, aside from my honeybun."

"And we managed to put away a killer." Mack crossed his arms over his exposed chest, but his thick, hairy legs were still on full display, which was not a glimpse I often got of my leather-clad friend.

"I don't think I've ever seen you two in bathing suits," I said, trying to keep my gaze on anything but their revealing Speedos. "I assumed they'd be black, like all your other clothes."

Buster glanced down at the sombrero-wearing llamacorn on the front of his formfitting spandex. "When in Rome."

Leatrice eyed the hefty man's tiny suit. "They dress like that in Rome?"

"I need to travel more," Fern murmured from his reclined position. "As long as our next trip doesn't involve being chased by a lunatic killer."

"This trip hasn't been all crazy killers," I said.

"You're right, sweetie." Fern arched an eyebrow at me. "One dead body per day for a bachelorette getaway is perfectly normal."

Mike lowered his head so he could whisper in my ear. "It's par for the course for your crew."

I nudged him playfully with my elbow. "Very funny."

He rubbed his side as if my jab had actually hurt. "Who was joking?"

Kate held up her hands. "Regardless of what happened so far, we still have a day or two of the trip left, and I, for one, am not going to waste a single moment of them."

Daniel grabbed her hand and pulled her up into an embrace, dipping her back and kissing her neck while her sunglasses fell to the grass. "Challenge accepted."

She laughed and swatted at him as he swooped her back up and onto her feet, but she was clearly pleased by his display of affection, and I was thrilled that her nerves or jitters or whatever had been bothering her about getting married seemed to have vanished.

"Technically, grooms aren't allowed at bachelorette parties," Richard said, but hurried forward with the rest of his statement when he saw Daniel frown, "but since this celebration has already broken so many rules, I suppose we can break a few more."

Daniel gave him an approving nod then scooped Kate's sunglasses from the grass and slid them onto her face. Sometimes, I had to remind myself that the silver fox ex-cop was actually engaged to my free-spirited assistant turned business partner, but I'd learned long ago that I wasn't a judge of what worked between couples. I was an expert on weddings, not marriage.

"I know I feel safer having two hot cops sleeping in the main house with us." Fern gave Daniel a long, drawn-out wink.

"Who's sleeping?" Kate said with a wicked smile as she stared up adoringly at her fiancé.

Leatrice released a mournful sigh. "All this talk has made me miss my love muffin, but I know he's busy with work."

"And dog sitting." Richard gave her a pointed look, no doubt imagining that Sidney Allen was treating Hermès' care like a full-time job.

"We'll be home soon enough," I reminded everyone. "Let's not think about DC or the work waiting for us when we get home. For now, we're still on island time."

"Which means it's always happy hour." Kate readjusted her sunglasses. "I think this day calls for a few margaritas."

Fern pushed himself off the lounger and started walking toward the driveway. "At the very least."

Leatrice hurried after him, and the rest of us fell in step more slowly. I cast a final glance at the luxurious house and its infinity pool. It might be impressive, but I much preferred our thatched roof house with more traditional Mexican details, and I was eager to get back to it and fall into bed.

"How's the baby doing after all the chaos?" Kate asked as she walked next to me, keeping her voice low enough that Richard couldn't hear.

She probably didn't need to worry since he was deeply engrossed in a conversation with my husband about the designer crib Richard had selected and when they should assemble it.

I rubbed my belly. "Not too bad. He or she seems to handle stress pretty well."

"How could it not, being the offspring of a detective and a wedding planner?" She threw her arm around my shoulders as her fiancé drifted off to talk to Buster and Mack about Harleys. "By the way, today wasn't a total disaster."

I eyed her and recognized that tone. She had something big to tell me. "It wasn't?"

She shook her head, clearly suppressing a huge grin. "Daniel and I decided on a wedding date."

I blew out a long breath. "Finally. What's the date? Not during one of our busy seasons, I hope."

She made a face like I was crazy to even suggest such a thing. "Of course not. You know how we don't take any weddings around Christmas or New Year's anymore?"

My pulse fluttered uneasily.

"That's why we decided on a New Year's Eve wedding." She gave my shoulders a squeeze. "Won't that be fun?"

"Fun," I repeated woodenly. I did quick mental math. By the last day in December, I would be almost nine months pregnant. What could possibly be more fun than that?

* * *

THANK you for reading *Day of the Wed*!

If you'd like to read a bonus Annabelle Archer short story, click the link below:

https://BookHip.com/XSZKPG

* * *

This book has been edited and proofed, but typos are like little gremlins that like to sneak in when we're not looking. If you spot a typo, please report it to: laura@lauradurham.com
Thank you!!

ALSO BY LAURA DURHAM

Annabelle Archer Series:
Better Off Wed
For Better Or Hearse
Dead Ringer
Review To A Kill
Death On The Aisle
Night of the Living Wed
Eat, Prey, Love
Groomed For Murder
Wed or Alive
To Love and To Perish
Marry & Bright
The Truffle with Weddings
Irish Aisles are Smiling
Godfather of Bride
Claus for Celebration
Bride or Die
Slay Bells Ring
Jewel of the Aisle
Day of the Wed

Annabelle Archer Books available as Audiobooks:
Better Off Wed
For Better Or Hearse
Dead Ringer

Review to a Kill

Annabelle Archer Collection: Books 1-4

Book 3

ABOUT THE AUTHOR

Laura Durham has been writing for as long as she can remember and has been plotting murders since she began planning weddings over twenty years ago. Her first novel, BETTER OFF WED, won the Agatha Award for Best First Novel.

When she isn't writing or wrangling brides, Laura loves traveling with her family, standup paddling, perfecting the perfect brownie recipe, and reading obsessively.

She loves hearing from readers and she would love to hear from you! Send an email or connect on social media (links below) .

Find me on:
www.lauradurham.com
laura@lauradurham.com

Copyright © 2023 by Broadmoor Books

Cover Design by Llewellen Designs

All rights reserved.

No part of this book may be reproduced in any form or by any electronic or mechanical means, including information storage and retrieval systems, without written permission from the author, except for the use of brief quotations in a book review.

This is a work of fiction. Names, characters, places, and incidents are the products of the author's imagination or are used fictitiously and are not to be construed as real. Any resemblance to actual events, locales, organizations, or persons, living or dead, is entirely coincidental.

Made in the USA
Monee, IL
29 October 2023